ONE BRIGHT STAR

Recent Titles by Suzanne Goodwin from Severn House

A RISING STAR
STARSTRUCK

ONE BRIGHT STAR

Suzanne Goodwin

This title first published in Great Britain 1998 by
SEVERN HOUSE PUBLISHERS LTD of
9–15 High Street, Sutton, Surrey SM1 1DF.
Originally published 1973 in Great Britain under the
title *To Seek A Star* and pseudonym of *Suzanne Ebel.*
First published in the USA 1998 by
SEVERN HOUSE PUBLISHERS INC., of
595 Madison Avenue, New York, NY 10022.

British Library Cataloguing in Publication Data

Goodwin,   Suzanne
          One bright star
          1.   Love stories
          1.   Title II. Ebel, Suzanne
          823.9'14 [F]

          ISBN 0-7278-5387-2

Printed and bound in Great Britain by
MPG Books Ltd, Bodmin, Cornwall.

I

Julie was first at the theatre that evening. She was relieved, when she pushed open the door of her dressing-room, to find that Tam Waring hadn't yet arrived.

Julie liked Tam very much and was touched by her friendliness; after all, Tam *was* famous. She was also the daughter of a world star. Few actresses in such a position would have been willing to share a very small dressing-room with an unknown Rep actress like Julie. Actors – those classless folk! – were usually sharply aware of one particular difference. And that was the difference between fame and insignificance. Tam Waring wasn't like that; she shared jokes as well as the tiny room with Julie; the two girls enjoyed each other's company. The short run of *Much Ado About Nothing* in which they were playing was going much too quickly, Julie thought.

But it was a relief to be alone sometimes. She had been playing Hero in *Much Ado* at the Sheridan Theatre for a week now and she was happy. It was the most important acting date she had yet had, just as the Sheridan was the best theatre she'd played in. The Sheridan was out of London but not so far distant that critics couldn't be persuaded to drive down and take a look at some of the productions.

This closeness to London was a reason why actresses as well known as Tamara Waring were glad to play there. An even stronger reason was the Sheridan's reputation, due to the woman who ran it, Margery Wylie. Miss Wylie made the Sheridan her life's work, spending every waking hour at her theatre and often sleeping in her office as well, 'so as not to waste time.'

'Her surname suits her,' Tam had remarked to Julie during the first week of rehearsals. 'Have you complained about your salary yet?'

'I wouldn't dare.'

'Pooh. She wanted you as Hero, everybody said so. But I bet she couldn't resist doing you down for a pound or two. Her meanness is a *legend*,' said Tam. 'And she won't spend a

5

bean on anything but her productions. I mean, us poor actors have to whistle, she spends the cash on sets and costumes. And look at this furniture – it hasn't seen a lick of paint since they built the place.'

It was true that the Sheridan, well run and usually packed, was shabby; Miss Wylie repaired but never replaced. The foyer carpet was re-sewn so that the worn bits were under the furniture or half hidden by curtains. The drop curtains were cunningly patched, and the 1930-style bar, decorated with pieces of looking-glass in patterns of fans, was carefully preserved : every time a morsel of glass fell out, it was put back with adhesive by Margery Wylie herself.

'She keeps the old place together with glue,' commented Tam. 'So remember one thing. It's wise to sit down very very carefully on any furniture at the Sheridan. Or you'll break your neck.'

Julie remembered this instruction as she sat down gingerly on the shabby sofa under the window.

The small dressing-room, like the rest of the Sheridan, was faded nineteen thirties. The chairs were knocked-about silver, the dressing-tables heavy and painted a yellowish pink. On the table the girls arranged their flowers, thumbed scripts of the play, copies of *The Stage* magazine. Other treasures were gradually accumulating – a large straw hat, a mangy old Koala bear, a black umbrella lined with crimson silk, and a plastic green toad of blissful expression holding a bunch of multi-coloured balloons.

Julie put her feet up. Leaning back, her arms behind her head, she thought about her rôle in this evening's perform-ance. The girl she played, Hero, was so young and happy and then – wronged and misjudged. Julie would *be* Hero in a little while; she would change from Julie Woods and put on the joys and sufferings of Shakespeare's young heroine. Hero's dresses hung nearby; Hero's curls were arranged on a wig-stand on the dressing-table. Hero's hopes and fears, loves and despairs, were waiting too.

The actress's life. You created it from inside you as a spider makes a web; it was as elaborate and ephemeral, as beautiful when covered with drops of rain, sometimes as fatal.

Julie was thin, on the small side, with a round face and large hazel eyes. Her expression was at times gentle and youthful, at times determined and even passionate. She had a large mouth which broke easily into a mischievous smile. She wore her brown hair rather long and she moved with light-

6

ness: she'd trained as a dancer at a ballet school.

Now she lay deep in thought about Shakespeare's *Much Ado About Nothing* and her own part of the young girl, Hero; Hero is a girl of the nobility, loved by Claudio and about to marry him. But he is wickedly misled into believing her unfaithful and wanton. He denounces her in the church on their wedding day – she faints and is thought to be dead. What must it be like to be disgraced, thrown over by your man while you stand there in your wedding dress? She'd thought this many, many times, recreating the scene of Hero's disgrace in her mind, peopling her imagination with the play's characters. With Claudio, the conventional young man of 'good family' so easily led to believe his love a whore. With Beatrice, the witty, impulsive girl who loved Hero and eventually rescued her . . . Julie lay lost in thought. The door burst open.

'Gracious, what's wrong, darling? Are you ill?'

Tam Waring, dressed in brilliant turquoise, came darting over to stare down at Julie. Tam had flaming red hair, a pale face sparkling with vitality and an expression of deep concern.

'You must be ill,' she announced.

'Tam,' protested Julie, putting out a hand which Tam disappointedly pronounced to be cool as a cucumber, 'I'm fine.'

'I don't see how you can be. What are you doing lying down at six in the evening? You are actually *reclining*. Women haven't done that since the French Empire and they only did it then because the dresses they wore looked seductive trailing off chaises longues . . . what are *you* doing it for?'

'I was thinking.'

'Then think standing up,' said Tam simply. 'If my father saw you like that he'd force you to take a bottleful of vitamins.'

'You make your famous Dad sound terrifying,' remarked Julie. Her time of reflection was clearly over and she stood up. 'A sort of Monster of the Lagoon.'

'That's right. Or a Night with the King Vampire.'

Tam unzipped her dress and pulled on a towelling dressing-gown. Julie also undressed, tied a gown round her, and the girls sat at the shabby dressing-tables which were side by side. Julie switched on the harsh unshaded lights which edged the mirrors.

'One cannot describe my father luridly enough,' muttered

7

Tam, critically examining her face. 'Just wait till you meet him.'

'I long to,' said Julie politely.

Neither girl spoke again, as they started to make up. As Julie painstakingly fixed on the enormous eyelashes like the antennae of an insect, which enlarged her eyes, painted her eyelids grey and blue, put emerald dots in the corners, rouged her cheekbones, she was thinking about Tam's father. The fact was that the one thing she did *not* want to do was to meet Sir Robert Waring.

It was, of course, lacking in intelligence on Julie's part not to jump at any chance to meet him. One of the most famous actors in the world, he also headed the Royalty Theatre, a permanent acting ensemble rivalling the National and the Royal Shakespeare. Tam often said, in her sudden way, 'I must introduce you to Sir.' Julie always thanked her and hoped devoutly it wouldn't happen.

Julie was the new girl, who was sometimes called 'the mouse of the Rep'. What happened when a mouse met a star? All she would get would be a smile and a hand-clasp, a sort of dismissive kindness; much worse to nerve herself to meet Sir and plummet into gloom because he thought nothing of her than never to meet him at all! Julie had made up her mind that at any time when there was the distant sound of Tam's famous father's famous voice, she – Julie – would quietly slip away and come back when he'd gone.

She finished her face and began to put on the pearl-threaded wig of long fair curls which she wore as Hero. Tam was busy winding intricate red plaits round her head and fixing on the outsized pearl and sapphire earrings which Beatrice wore in Act I.

Julie met Tam's eye in the looking-glass.

'How do you suppose your favourite leading man will be tonight?' Julie said, speaking of Tam's opposite number, an actor called John Locking who played Benedick.

Locking was tall and thin and looked like a crane or a stork. He was patronizing and conceited, with a cold manner off-stage.

'Perhaps he'll warm up a bit,' Julie said comfortingly.

Tam sighed. 'Locking couldn't be "warmed up", as you call it, if we gave him one of those charcoal thingies they hold in their laps in Tibet. He's a fish on the slab. Imagine. A Benedick of cold haddock. Ugh.'

'He isn't as bad as that.'

8

'Oh yes, he is. You'll have to get out of that habit of seeing the best in everyone, you know. It's a hard, cruel world we're in, darling!' said Tamara, stepping into a dress of softest yellow silk, flowing with ribbons and pearls.

Julie fastened on her own heavy white silk costume for Act I and took some time fiddling with her wig. Tam watched and offered advice.

Tam was the girl who took over a friend's problems and solved them whether the friend liked it or not. Julie didn't appear to have many to solve; Tam thought this a pity.

The girls were ready now. They turned towards each other, magically transformed, Tam stately in a yellow robe of trailing draperies, Julie in virginal white with a diaphanous lace fan. They sat down, costumes falling into sculpted folds.

Tam said, 'What news today, darling?'

She made this kindly enquiry because she knew Julie was worried about what happened when *Much Ado* finished its short run. Every actress starts worrying about her next play before the present one finishes.

'Oh, everything's all right,' Julie said cheerfully. 'I wrote ten letters today and I've used up all my photographs so I've ordered twelve more. I also reminded my agent to try and get someone to come down and see *Much Ado* before it finishes.'

Tam looked impressed. 'Ten letters. That's a lot. But how do you feel? I hope you're not getting fussed and starting the what-am-I-going-to-do-next syndrome, Julie. One must get hardened.'

'Oh I know. I am already,' lied Julie.

Tam stared abstractedly at her own hand which was loaded with huge rings meant to be seen from the back of the upper circle.

'I wish you had something settled,' she said. 'I know just how you feel, even though I haven't been churning out letters every day to directors and casting people and agents and things. But that's only because I'm lucky enough to be married to a man who writes marvellous plays with parts for me.'

'Not true. You're a good actress.'

'No better than you are.'

'Tam. That was kind. I actually believe you mean it.'

'Of course I do,' said Tam, laughing. 'I couldn't say that to an actress unless she was super, could I? I've been thinking. My David knows a lot of useful people you ought to

9

meet. And you and I really must fix up for you to see Sir. We keep talking about it.'

'It's very sweet of you and don't think I'm not grateful,' Julie said, rather too quickly. 'But I can manage. Truly. I've a very good agent. And . . . somehow it doesn't seem right to pull strings.'

Tam was genuinely astounded. She stared at Julie with her mouth open. 'Everybody uses influence,' she exclaimed, 'if they happen to *have* any! My poor girl –'

She was about to launch into a speech when, to Julie's relief, the intercom loudspeaker announced : 'Four minutes. Four minutes.' The music of the dance which opened and closed *Much Ado* began to play; it was the signal for the girls to get ready for their entrance. As the music weaved its formal patterns they rose in a single sweeping movement, and Julie felt Hero's emotions and loves begin to stir in her mind.

The girls rustled out of the room; yellow dress and white, red hair and brown, the famous girl and the unknown, walked down the stone stairs together towards the brilliantly lit stage.

The Sheridan audiences were usually receptive, and the performance tonight went with a swing. The play itself, *Much Ado*, with its story of 'wooing, wedding and repenting', was a favourite with audiences. They enjoyed the word-fencing of Beatrice and Benedick. Love, in the play, was the subject of the liveliest quarrels. And then there was the dramatic turn of the plot, the seeming death of Hero, her return to her lover, and that blissfully happy, dancing end. Tamara Waring playing the teasing, witty Beatrice was an added attraction; the public knew and loved her already. She had inherited some of her father's unmistakable magic. So the Sheridan's *Much Ado* was already sold out for its limited run.

This evening, as the play raced by and Julie heard the audience laugh or felt them breathlessly silent, she enjoyed the performance intensely. Even Tam's 'cold haddock', John Locking, seemed good and, during one of his soliloquies, when Tam and Julie were standing in the wings together, Julie thought she actually detected a gleam on Tam's face that might be approval.

'John Locking wasn't so bad, was he?' whispered Julie after they'd passed him and he'd given them a friendly salute.

'I shall have to consider that,' said Tam, who rarely

changed verdicts without hearing the case all over again. Suddenly she gave a shriek of delight and started to run down the corridor. A man was walking ahead of them. Tam caught him up, threw her arms round his neck and kissed him passionately. It was the kind of joyous, wild greeting, thought Julie, you see at airports. You certainly wouldn't guess that Tam had seen her husband a few hours before.

Julie hesitated, thinking she would slip away to the Green Room for a coffee and give Tam a chance to have David to herself. When Tam's husband was around, Julie felt in the way. Tam was so wildly in love it was quite cruel to be there at all.

But as Julie turned to go, Tam exclaimed, 'Don't creep off in that heavily tactful way, Julie Woods! You know I go on like this all the time. Can I help it if he's gorgeous?'

David Bryden, his wife still clinging to him, grinned at Julie in a friendly way and congratulated her on tonight's performance.

'It went well tonight and you were lovely. By the way, Tam and I want you to have supper with us. You will, won't you?'

David Bryden was an attractive, lively man, with thick hair of a darker copper than Tam's, and freckles. His face had the mobility of a comedian's. Julie liked him, but she had the young actress's awe of successful playwrights. It was not like being an actor whose work she understood intuitively; she found the making of a play a mystery.

'Tam and I are going to a new place, a farmhouse I discovered the other day when I was driving around. It's on the river, and the food is good. You'll like it,' David said.

Julie hesitated. 'But are you sure –'

'Absolutely certain!' chimed in Tam.

David left the girls at their dressing-room door, telling them to hurry. Soon the girls had discarded their elaborate costumes, altering in a few minutes from figures of 16th-century Italian nobility to English girls of the '70s. It was a miraculous change neither of them noticed as they laid aside wigs sewn with pearls and zipped up flimsy cotton dresses.

'I'm glad you decided to come, Julie,' said Tam, as they walked out into the warm night street.

Was there a slight note of satisfaction in her voice rather . . . Julie thought . . . as if Tam had won some little game they'd been playing? Julie looked at her. Tam's face was smooth as cream.

David's open sports car was parked under a street lamp near the stage door and suddenly Julie, looking over at the car, thought: Oh *lor*.

It wasn't only David who was waiting for them; there was another young man in the car as well.

Who's he? thought Julie, spirits dropping.

Tam darted over to the car and chatted to both men and beckoned Julie who followed, thinking nostalgically of coffee in the Green Room and a gossip with one of the company.

'Here she is. Looking delicious, don't you think?' announced Tam in a proprietary manner Julie didn't exactly relish. 'Julie, this is Daniel. Dan – Julie. He saw the play tonight, by the way.'

'Hallo.'

The young man seated at the back of the car half stood up to shake her hand. Julie climbed into the back and sat beside him and a moment later the car set off on a fast flight through the town, out into the open country.

'I liked your Hero very much,' said Julie's companion.

Julie thanked him and added shyly, 'The production's good, isn't it?'

'So so. You and Tam are the best things in it. The Locking man is awful.'

'Oh, no, surely.'

'It's no good being loyal about him. He made Benedick a bore,' said Daniel, laughing. 'I've seen Locking before and he's getting worse, it must be that TV success. Much more interesting is how I've managed to miss seeing you before now. I'm always in the theatre. Why haven't I seen you?'

'I've only been in Rep.'

'But I'm always watching Rep and some of it is great. Where have you been?'

'Wales. The Midlands.'

He waited for her to elaborate – actresses love to talk about themselves. But Julie said nothing else, and so he asked her where she had trained.

'At ballet school, as a matter of fact.'

'How did you switch from dance to drama?' he asked, intrigued.

'It was chance, really,' she said. 'I was in a play in which the dancer – me – had a speaking part. And then later I found myself doing more acting than dancing. It sort of happened; it wasn't planned.'

Her companion said the same kind of things had hap-

12

pened to him – momentous things based on chance.

She was interested in the man sitting beside her in the close proximity of the narrow car. Who was he? She tried to remember if Tam had talked about anybody called Daniel. Probably not : Tam usually talked about friends in the mass, using collective nouns.

'Everybody rang,' Tam would say, or : 'Twenty characters descended on us at the week-end.'

Glancing at her companion, Julie said tentatively, 'You must be an actor so how have *I* missed seeing you?'

'I've never been an actor, Julie.'

She liked the way he called her by her name. 'Then you must be a playwright like David.'

'I couldn't write plays to save my life,' he said, laughing.

'Try twenty questions. Start at the beginning.'

Julie, amused, said promptly, 'Well. First point is that you're obviously in the theatre.'

'Why is it obvious? I'll take that up later. However, the answer's yes.'

'Not an actor. Not a dramatist.' She reflected. 'A director, then?'

He shook his head.

'Stage managing? Lighting? Choreography?'

'No to all three.'

She studied him, frowning, and he returned the look triumphantly.

'What is left?' she said. 'Music? No. I know! You arrange fights . . . the ones in *Hamlet* and the Histories and in films and on TV. *Do* you arrange fights?'

'You're looking so pleased that I feel quite sorry to say I don't.'

'What a shame. I've always wanted to meet someone who does that. So. No fencing foils?'

'I wouldn't say that.'

'A clue! Fencing foils. Fencing foils . . .' She considered for a while and then said, 'Golly, *I* don't know.'

'I'll give you another clue. I didn't approve of those thick black veils you were smothered in during Act Three.'

'*A designer*! Of course!' She suddenly remembered a set design which Tam had shown her, a wonderful, ingenious arrangement of metal rods and projections. 'You've just designed David's new play.'

'Still working on it. It isn't finished yet,' Daniel said.

'What a gorgeous job,' said Julie thoughtfully. Like every

13

actor, she knew how important costume and set could be. Like few actors, the actual work itself, the creation of design, fascinated her.

'It's nice to hear you say so,' he said. 'Actors can get very angry with designers. Or feel let down by them. The designer and the actor have a very odd relationship. Incidentally, I wish I had been given the chance to design your costumes in *Much Ado.*'

'I wish you'd had a go at mine,' put in Tam, who had turned round in the car, leaning over with her arm in front of her like a child looking over a fence. 'My costume in the "Kill Claudio" scene is death. Dan, do you think I could do anything about it? I thought I might chop off the sleeves and get the girl in the wardrobe to sew lace on. Or dye it.'

'Tamara, is that the way you treat the poor unfortunate designer's work?' said Daniel. 'Let me catch you chopping off the sleeves of one of my costumes.'

'Pooh. Yours are worth wearing,' said Tam airily.

The car slowed down and turned into a narrow lane, almost a cart track, winding beside a little river overgrown with rushes. They drew to a stop and David switched off the engine. Julie noticed how the night silence flooded over them. Then he switched off the headlights and they were left in the silent radiance of a night without stars.

'I can't see a thing,' announced Tam, getting out of the car. 'Are you sure this is the right road, David darling? There isn't a barn within miles.'

'The restaurant's at the end of the lane to the right. I'd rather not take the car any farther; the ground's too muddy and we might get stuck,' said David. 'Be careful how you walk. Let's hurry or they'll think we are not coming and close the kitchen.'

'But Julie and I are starving!' cried Tam in the voice of every actress after a successful performance.

Daniel took Julie's hand as they set off up the lane. David and Tam's dim shapes were ahead of them. The wind rustled in the rushes, the air smelled of the river and the damp fields. Julie was beginning to get her night sight. She saw masses of small white flowers on the river bank, and in marshy ground were the juicy stems and yellow discs of kingcups.

Tam's voice in the distance called, 'Food!'

Daniel guided Julie round the corner of the lane: they came on a transformation scene.

Under a row of elms were a number of parked cars near

14

a low-built comfortable farmhouse which glowed with lights. The river ran at the edge of the farmhouse garden and an ancient apple tree bent over the water; somebody had wound its crooked branches with a necklace of white lights like magic fruit among the leaves.

'Lovely,' Julie said and at the same time : 'Beautiful,' murmured Daniel.

'You are *clever*!' Tam said to her husband. 'Let's hurry before they lock up the scampi.'

Inside the farmhouse was a large, pleasant room with a stone floor and scrubbed wooden tables. The room, the house, were unmistakably English. The *maître d'hôtel* was infinitely Spanish. He was beaky, black-haired, with the air of an aristocrat in disguise. He showed them to a corner table with a grave bow and presented them with a menu written in flowing Spanish.

David Bryden was amused as they chose their meal.

'Isn't it funny? Nice and funny. England's love affair with the Continent pops up in the most unexpected places. That's why I wanted us to come here.'

'Spain in an English lane edged with kingcups and a farmhouse where they used to make curds and whey,' Daniel said.

Julie enjoyed the dinner party. She had not wanted to come out with David and Tam and she'd wanted it even less when she had seen there was a fourth member of the party, a man she didn't know. She was young and attractive and enjoyed meeting new men but not if she suspected she was being introduced so that someone could do her a good turn. That was what she guessed Tam was up to. But this reluctance to be a lame duck of Tam's was forgotten as she sat beside Daniel and enjoyed the meal and the conversation.

Her friend Tam reminded Julie this evening of those fireworks called sparklers. Quite a fountain of sparks, a positive bunch of sizzling flowers, capable of burning the carpet. She was sparkling away with her husband and Daniel watching, and Daniel disagreeing with what she said.

'I tell you, Daniel, designers make *fearful* mistakes about colours. I don't care if colour is the designer's province or not, he can do the most terrible things! How about the man I worked with who took an actress with red hair – me! – and put her in a set of exactly the same colour? Didn't the moron realize that when I stood in his horrible set I became *completely bald*! I was forced to wear an ash-blonde wig and then I looked like a tightrope walker.'

15

'What do you think, Julie?' asked Daniel, laughing.

'I – I think she's probably right.'

There was a chorus of jeers at this feeble reply and Tam said, 'All right, I admit I talk too much. I go on and on and in the end nobody listens. Julie switched off and it's my fault. Darling David, why don't you shut me up?'

'Darling Tam, I do try.'

She made a wonderful face at him.

During coffee at the end of the meal, Tam said, 'David, it's no good putting it off any longer, we've *got* to ring Sir about the week-end or he'll kill us. Let's go and get it over.'

'But isn't it too late?' David said, looking at his watch. 'One thing I'd hate would be to wake your father up.'

'Pooh. He won't be asleep, you surely know that by now. He's a night bird. An owl. A bird of prey. At his predatory best at three in the morning. It's horrible to think about it,' said Sir's daughter. 'Come on, darling.'

She and David crossed the restaurant and Julie found herself for the first time that evening alone with Daniel. There was that little embarrassed pause that happens when strangers who share mutual friends are left on their own. Julie wondered who would speak first.

After a moment Daniel said reflectively, 'Good.'

'What is?'

'Getting you alone for a moment. Without Tam dead centre stage with every light blazing.'

'But she's – '

'Sensational. I agree. She also inhibits conversation. One is forced into the rôle of audience whether one likes it or not. That's why I argue with her, so as to stop it being a solo turn. By the way, when am I going to see you again?'

The sentence, casually added at the end of his teasing remarks about Tam, took Julie by surprise.

'Oh. I don't know.'

'Come out with me some time this week, Julie. Will you?'

'I – I'd like to,' she said.

He looked pleased and said, 'Thank you. I'll telephone you at the theatre. You mustn't think I am not devoted to Tam,' he went on, smiling. 'Who can resist her? It is just that I would like a little more of Julie. Do you realize I know nothing about you?'

He leaned forward slightly, his chin on his hand. Julie thought that this was a fascinating man. His mouth was a beautiful shape, his skin pale and sallow, she liked his eyes

16

which were so dark they were almost black. There were a lot of replies you could give to such a leading male question. You could give come-on replies, or put-off ones; you could be flirtatious or sexy; you could be rather vain because a man was clearly interested in you. She said, 'I know nothing about you either.'

'Then let's find out,' Daniel said.

Just then there was a flash of blue and a sudden laugh, and Tam came swinging back towards them.

The radio was playing pop with such a fast beat that Julie didn't hear the knock on her door. It opened and a curly head peered round, followed by a boyish figure in baggy jeans and a brown sweater with a hole in the sleeve.

'Julie, can I come and join you for a bit?' asked Christopher, carrying his breakfast tray into her room and sitting down on the bed. 'May I eat my boiled egg with you? You did say I could come and call when I felt a bit low and this morning I'm at rock bottom.'

Julie picked up her nail file and nail polish, sat down on a wicker stool near Christopher. She always liked seeing him. Apart from Tam, Chris was her closest friend at the Sheridan. She'd known Chris for two years, and he and she had worked in Rep together a couple of times before.

Chris was twenty-one and his job was Assistant Stage Manager. His appearance, however, was nothing to do with managing anything. He looked as if he had arrived straight from a forest inhabited by Greek gods and goddesses. Julie often thought she could imagine Chris sitting on a green sward playing a reed pipe, or as an assistant to Bacchus and his revellers. His ears would have to be a little more pointed, and his eyes a fraction more slanting, and then he would *be* a creature from the Golden Age. When she told Chris how she imagined him, he agreed.

'People have said it before. A young satyr. Or a faun or something. I'd be dashing in hot pursuit of a luscious nymph, wouldn't I?'

'Exactly.'

'Well, you know, that's what I do. I'm always running after girls, Julie.'

'But do you catch them, Chris?'

'Of course.'

It was Chris who, practised at the art, had found the best digs in the town, and had taken a room for Julie as well as for himself. Sharing digs, Chris could haunt her room and talk her into making him cups of instant coffee with Julie's electric kettle. He would also arrive with little offerings of chocolate or oranges, which he would divide into exact halves before they settled down to talk shop.

Chris was good at shop and always up-to-the-minute with the news. Now, buttering toast and complaining about the small amount of marmalade doled out by Mrs Thing, he said, 'What news of the Big Man's daughter?'

'Nothing much. Should there be?'

'You are maddening, Julie. You went out with her and Bryden last night; I saw you driving away in that Porsch or whatever it was. What did you all talk about?'

'I can't remember. Oh yes, I can. Design.'

He looked at her mischievously, his freckled face, with its pointed chin and a crown of curly brown hair, malicious.

'I notice you've omitted the fact that there was a fourth member of the party. Dan Monteith. Did you fancy him, Julie? He's attractive, wouldn't you say?'

'Daniel Monteith is very nice and rather handsome and you shut up,' she said. '*Please*, Chris!'

'Oh, all right. I do like teasing you but I'll lay off for the time being,' he said, crunching his toast. 'Anyway, I didn't come to hear about you hob-nobbing with the famous but to tell you that I've got some news about you and me. It isn't particularly good, so fasten your seat belt.'

Julie, who had been painting her thumb-nail carefully, gave a sudden start and let the nail polish smudge.

'Yes. It's what you're thinking, Julie. I was in Margery Wylie's office last night, chatting up that new bird from the box office, and I happened to see the casting for next month's play. They're doing an early Coward piece, I forget its name. And you and I have been included *out*.'

Silence.

He said, 'Cheer up! We said we weren't expecting anything, didn't we?'

Julie went over to the window. She gazed down into the street where a fine, steady rain was falling, making the pavements shine black.

Chris looked at her back turned to him and said nothing. He'd lived all his twenty-one years in this atmosphere of frustrated hope. Both his parents were actors. Chris himself had started to act but found he had no talent. Secretly he wanted to become a theatre director, but how to achieve this

18

ambition? He stayed in the only world he cared about and
went from job to job as a not very efficient ASM, relying on
his quickness and charm to get by when he forgot prompts
or props. Secretly, he worked over a tattered copy of a
forgotten Victorian melodrama he'd found in an old book-
shop months ago on a tour. He was going to direct it and turn
it into a romping farce. 'And when I do, *you* shall be my
lead,' he told Julie.

He loved Julie but she was not one of the nymphs she
chased. She was in a different category for Chris; she was
a friend. He loved the way she looked, she was so small and
graceful, her face round like a child's, her voice slightly
hoarse, her hands expressive. He liked her figure, the clothes
she wore, her small feet, her scent, her cautious temperament,
her willingness to laugh. But he never ran after her.

Now he poured himself another cup of tea and philosophically added six lumps of sugar.

'I know the casting director at Chichester. Let's ring him
and see if we can get an appointment,' he suggested. 'I'll ring
today, shall I?'

Julie turned round, her expression cheerful again. 'Yes, do,
Chris. But can you really mention me too?'

'I shall mention you *first*. He'll have heard about your good
notices. Things like that travel fast,' said Chris. 'I'll let you
know what happens.'

He finished his breakfast, the rain continued to fall in a
drenching mist over the town, and Julie recovered her good
spirits. She set her mind back into its usual philosophical
channels : after all, it was stupid even to expect another part
at the Sheridan. Everybody knew that Margery Wylie liked
to change her actors all the time. And just because Julie's
notices had been good, it didn't follow that Miss Wylie would
immediately go back on her own policy, did it? It was absurd
to be depressed, she told herself. Look how calmly Chris
was taking it!

He stood up, holding the tray, and said, 'Thank you for the
company. Can I bring my breakfast in again? See you at the
understudy rehearsal. It's in twenty minutes – I must fly – '

Julie smiled after he'd gone. Chris cheered her up. For if it
was true that misfortunes were halved by being shared,
Chris's situation and her own were comfortingly similar.
Both had a job that was going to last precisely three more
weeks. Both had not been offered the chance to stay on at
the Sheridan, despite *Much Ado*'s success. Both were under

twenty-four, had less than £10 in the Post Office and parents who couldn't afford to help them.

Julie opened her wardrobe, took out a mackintosh and tied a scarf round her head. She'd lent Tam her umbrella days ago. Looking out of the window to see exactly how heavy the rain was, she put on a second scarf. She ran downstairs just as Chris, shouting 'I have to be there ten minutes before the actors. I'm flying!' whirled out of his room in a cape, and set off up the road.

Chris disappeared round the corner and Julie pushed her hands into her mackintosh pockets and walked up the damp street, fast but not running. The street was crowded with shoppers but she scarcely noticed them, for she was thinking about Daniel. She had remembered him and their meeting and created him again in her imagination the moment she woke this morning. He was much too new and too interesting not to have made a strong impression.

Now like a welcomed visitor Daniel came back into her mind. She remembered his face, dark eyes, rather seductive way of talking. She wondered when – if – they were going to meet again. He had said, 'I'll call you.' Oh, would he? Part of her was certain they were going to see each other again, but the other prudent side of Julie prepared itself for disappointment. The same part of her mind that was schooled when jobs fell through, to stay hopeful, now counselled her not to hope much of Daniel Monteith. He was in the Waring-Bryden world, he certainly wasn't in hers. She and Chris were the other kind of theatre people, the ones who rang their agents every day hoping for work, using the casual formula that means so much more than it says : 'Any news?'

The stage door was jostling with damp actors shaking outsized umbrellas and engaging each other in vivacious conversation. The stage doorkeeper took no notice of anybody and was intent on brewing himself a steamy pot of tea. As Julie came briskly into the theatre the first person she saw, leaning against the wall, was Daniel.

She was surprised, and a little rush of pleasure made her heart race.

Daniel shouldered his way across to her. 'Good morning, Julie. I'm reliably informed by the guy over there who's pouring out that crimson tea that your rehearsal breaks at midday. Can I take you to lunch?'

'Oh yes. Thank you.'

She looked up and beamed at him and Daniel thought how

funny and beautiful she looked, like a drenched kitten, her hair glued to her forehead with rain and two dripping scarves stuck to her head.

'I'll be here waiting,' he said. 'I won't keep you now. You look a bit pushed.'

'Yes, I'm late. 'Bye – ' she said. She ran up to her dressing-room fast, burst in to find Tam already in practice clothes, a floor-length black skirt and polo necked sweater. Tam was tying up her red hair with a green ribbon.

'You're late! Julie, the punctual one. Late at last. It makes a nice change,' Tam said triumphantly.

'I know,' said Julie, hastily unbuttoning her mackintosh. 'But Daniel was at the stage door and – '

'Asked you for a date. Hooray.'

Julie, now pulling off her sweater, emerged from it pink in the face and said, 'Tam, I hope you didn't ask him to ask me, because if so – '

'Pooh! You don't know Daniel if you think *that* would work. Stop being suspicious when things go right for you, you idiot, and come *on*. Margery will eat us alive!'

It was part of theatre discipline, rigid as that of a ballet school in Leningrad, that actors were punctual for calls. They arrived on stage as the clock struck the appointed hour. Even in this small Rep theatre which most of the actors would have left in three weeks' time, punctuality was demanded and obeyed.

This morning the girls were four minutes late for the call, Tam having loyally stayed behind until Julie was ready. They slipped unobtrusively on to the stage and stood at the back with a band of actors in front of them.

The plan didn't work.

Margery Wylie, the grey-haired doyenne of the Sheridan, sitting in the stalls smoking French cigarettes, gave a loud accusing shout.

'Waring! Woods!'

The girls came meekly to the front of the stage.

'You're late,' shouted Margery Wylie. 'That's the second time, Waring. Persistent offenders cannot expect to get off scot-free. Next time I shall impose the Sheridan Fine! Right. Props? Where are props?'

Christopher's elfin face appeared; he was carrying an enormous branch of green paper leaves. Margery Wylie scolded him fiercely for not arranging the branch in a new position she'd decided upon. The rehearsal began.

Margery Wylie was as punctual as a clock, and the rehearsal finished at exactly midday. Julie hurried off the stage, leaving Tam giggling with Chris.

As she changed back into her dampish sweater and skirt, combed her hair and stared at herself critically in the glass, Julie did wish she was wearing better clothes. Her best, in fact. Julie had two bests, one of which she'd worn out to dinner last night. It was boring to be broke when one wanted to look good. She made a grimace at the glass, said, 'Woods, you look a mess,' and ran down the stairs, jumping the last few steps like a schoolgirl.

There he was. Daniel. Standing exactly where she'd left him, two and a half hours ago. He was reading a newspaper but the moment she came round the corner he looked up and said, 'Hallo.' He took her arm, saying he'd left the car outside and that the rain had stopped.

'The performance isn't until 7.30. What time do I have to deliver you back here?'

Daniel's car was long and low, rather like David Bryden's except that Daniel's was dark blue instead of black. He settled her into it, slammed the small door and came round to join her. The engine roared as the expensive car slipped down the street. Julie thought ruefully: 'How rich these people are.' She knew it was ridiculous but the thought didn't please her. What was Chris's old phrase about Tam? 'She's out of our league.' So was Bryden and so was Daniel Monteith. Julie had been in the theatre three years but nobody had driven her away from the stage door before in a car like this. The situation was the same with Tam; however much she might treat Julie as if they were in the same boat, they were not. Their boats were in different oceans at different ends of the world. And the only reason Tam was at the Sheridan at all was because it gave her the coveted chance to play Beatrice, Shakespeare's witty heroine . . .

'You're very quiet,' murmured Daniel, as the car drove away from the town and in the direction of a range of wooded hills misty in the greyish light of midday.

'I was thinking about Tam.'

'Well, don't. *I* want your attention today.'

Julie hoped he wasn't going to take her to another expensive restaurant. Her thoughts made her conscious of her old mackintosh. She had developed to a degree the actress's desire to look beautiful – to look her best. All women had this but in the actress's case it was part of her work more than natural feminine vanity. Julie did not fancy walking across some expensive dining-room wearing her old black and white dress, or handing her mackintosh to someone to hang up among a lot of commuter-type mink.

'I'm driving out of town because I don't want us to meet a lot of your friends who'll start talking theatre shop,' said Daniel. 'I know a pub where they'll cook us steak if we ask nicely.'

Julie was relieved.

The pub, called the Pair of Gloves, was an old-fashioned house in a quiet road lined with elm trees. The bar had panelled walls dark from wood-smoke and – a welcome sight on a wet day – a small wood fire crackling in an old black-leaded grate. The place was deserted except for two farmers bent over a paper and a man at the bar, sleeves rolled up, vigorously polishing a pewter tankard. The radio droned football scores.

'Good morning, Mister Monteith,' said the barman as Daniel came in.

'Good morning, Mister Vincent. Any hope of some steak?'

'I'll ask Mrs Vincent.'

The bartender disappeared through a curtained alcove, Daniel took Julie over to the fire and drew her a wheel-backed chair. Soon Mister Vincent returned with freshly cooked steak and chips. Daniel and Julie drank a glass of red wine, sat by the fire and talked. There was something kind as well as attractive about this big handsome young man, with his thick glossy hair and humorous mouth that curled at the corners. His skin was sallow, he had a nose that could have been classic except that it had a bump as if someone had punched it once. His chin was cleft, and when he laughed his cheeks had lines like little gashes on either side of his face.

Mister Vincent came to take their plates away. He looked approving when he saw that they'd eaten everything. He returned with home-made apple pie and cream.

'Tam would be deeply shocked if she saw us eating this,' said Julie.

'Tam's slimming kick is compulsive,' said Daniel. 'I don't know how David can bear it. When he and I dined out with her the other evening, all she would eat was raw vegetables and black coffee.'

'She says her new rôle in the Bryden play calls for a girl who weighs about seven stone,' said Julie, and Daniel laughed

23

and said, 'Rubbish. She likes to think that.'

There was a moment's silence. Julie said, 'She hasn't told me about the play but I did see your design for the set. Have you done the costumes yet? Could I see them, perhaps?'

'I'd like to show them to you. Are you coming to London soon?'

'Not till the end of the run.'

'What are you doing after *Much Ado* closes?'

The pause was long and noticeable.

'I'm not doing anything,' Julie said at last.

Daniel sighed. 'I know, I know, I'm breaking the unwritten law by asking you. I realize quite well, Julie, that it's bloody difficult to tell somebody you don't know where your next job is coming from. But you don't have to mind telling *me*. And I'm not going to start being heavily tactful with you; it would be too stupid. So I gather, from your doleful little face, that you were hoping Old Mother Wylie was going to offer you a part in her forthcoming Noel Coward production?'

'I suppose it's pathetically obvious that's what I would have loved. And I'm pathetically obvious.'

'Do you mind?'

'I suppose I do. I don't want to make people feel sorry for me, Daniel. That's the last thing I want. What I'd like is to stay cool and not show how much I mind. I hope I learn.'

'Well, I hope you don't. I like people to show their feelings; that's because I show mine all the time,' he said. 'You should see me getting angry when I argue with a director sometimes . . .'

Tactfully, without an obvious break, he started to talk about his own work. Julie was glad to listen. She'd never known a designer before except to say good morning to. Sometimes a harassed young man, in one or other of the theatres where she'd worked, had talked to her about her costume. But she had never had a friend who was a designer, and the idea of Daniel's work was fascinating.

They talked about the designer's problem of turning a play into three dimensions. The actor breathes life into the written words and turns the rôle into a man; the designer puts the man in clothes that say something about him; the designer creates his world – a room, a city, a forest, a cell – where the man lives and hopes and loves and suffers.

'Sometimes we start off with textures and colours – a tree perhaps, or a wall that creates an enclosed world. These things become the vocabulary we work in; one piece of stuff turns out to be right, another is wrong. Finally the overall picture is formed. I always want to keep the design fluid during rehearsal time but it's never possible. There's never time to design again *after* rehearsals have been on a few weeks. So it's vital to have a strong conception of the whole play from the beginning, and mould the details and develop them during rehearsals . . .'

'Tell me about the actors. Do they affect you a lot?'

'Sometimes. I once worked with Periandra Pratt, do you know her? She's one of Sir Robert Waring's favourite actresses.'

'I've seen her play.'

'She's brilliant, isn't she? But a sacred monster. Men are terrified of her. I was working on the sets and costumes of a play in which Periandra was the lead; she had to attempt suicide in Act One. I designed a dressing-gown for her. It was blue. Very straight with strong lines. Sombre. Periandra couldn't stand it. She said it was too boutique and hadn't any pockets. She said : "I want big worn-out pockets that the woman keeps her aspirin bottles in." Periandra didn't tell me but she went off to a cheap shop that was selling up old lines of clothes. You know the kind of thing. "Prices slashed". Periandra found a fearful old red dressing-gown with a tie belt and long braided lapels. She kept saying "Isn't it marvellous?" like a girl with a superb new dress. She was right. When I saw her play the scene in it, she was right.'

'Do the designer and the writer collaborate?' asked Julie, thinking about David Bryden and how he and Daniel had seemed on the same wave-length the evening before.

'Oh. Essentially. Ideally, you work together very early on – David and I have done on two of his plays. I worked on the one he did last year about Chatterton. The director and the designer work together as well. The production isn't complete until everything that's designed is used in movement, taken right into the production, made to *happen* . . . and I'm talking too much,' he finished, laughing.

'But I *love* shop. It's the best conversation. Tell me about David's new play.'

Daniel rubbed his nose and said it was a tough play to tackle because it mixed reality and fantasy, and the public never really took to fantasy. They liked recognizing themselves and their lives in what they saw.

'They love Shakespeare. But even the greatest work is re-interpreted for every generation,' he said. 'And Shakespeare's real life too. David's new play is definitely *not*.'

Julie said thoughtfully that she had always imagined people liked to get away from real life, not to be faced with it in the theatre.

Daniel shook his head.

'We do want to get away. But not into cloud cuckoo land. We want our dreams to be possible. We want to see beautiful things that – just – might happen. Everybody's daydreams are based on some kind of truth. Mine, for instance. I always imagine one day I'll design a huge great film epic. Ben Hur. Some Roman piece of work – super colossal. I'd love that. Just once. I don't mean I want to be hooked into epic after epic. I'd like to do a single one and do it superbly. It would fascinate me to extend one's scale from twenty feet of stage to twenty miles in a plain in Hungary or Northern India.'

Julie looked pensively at the fire; it had burned down to a feathery mass of ash, sweet-smelling but without flame. The farmers had gone and so had Mister Vincent, Daniel and she were alone. The rain had stopped and a watery sunlight gleamed through the window.

'What's your dream based on the just-possible?' Daniel asked.

'I don't know . . . yes, I do. To be a famous actress, I suppose. But that's ridiculous!'

'I would call that a very possible dream indeed.'

'Don't say that! It couldn't be true,' she exclaimed. 'I'm superstitious and I don't want to tempt fate! And it's quite *im*possible that I'll make the big time. What would be wonderful would be a small part in a big Company and the chance to play in real Repertory and do good work.'

Her manner was rather solemn, above all it was cautious, and her little voice, with its note of hoarseness, was touching. He said gently, 'You ought to allow yourself the luxury of hoping on a slightly larger scale, Julie.'

'Sometimes I don't allow myself to hope at all. Just to be glad and surprised when good things come along. But I suppose it *would* be a treat not to have to write ten letters every day!'

It was only after she'd spoken that she realized Daniel might think this was a hint for help. She was embarrassed but could think of no way of taking back what she'd said.

It was early evening when Daniel finally drew up at the stage door and they said goodbye.

They had spent the afternoon driving through the country, and Daniel had taken her to a Roman villa he found marked on an ordnance survey map. They were shown into a small place, a Roman gentleman's country house, and stood admiring a wonderful Roman pavement. Huge eyes in pale Roman cheeks stared up at them from a mosaic set in the uneven ground. 'Almost,' said Daniel, 'as if it was a piece of crumpled silk instead of mosaic.'

'There's a character from your Roman epic,' murmured Julie.

They had tea at a little house with rain-wet cabbage roses in the garden, and as they drove back to the theatre they sang pop songs, the words of which they discovered they both knew by heart.

As Julie said goodbye, Daniel took her hand and gave it a quick kiss.

'It was gorgeous. *You* are gorgeous. I'll telephone you tomorrow from London. We must meet again as soon as possible. Goodbye for today, lovely Julie.'

She went into the theatre and up to her dressing-room, the words of the song they'd been singing still repeating themselves in her head. 'Oh, just say. Yeah, just say. So much you have to tell me. Much you have to tell me.'

What had she and Daniel to tell each other?

She was surprised to find Tamara already in their dressing-room and, more surprising still, already in her Act One costume. Wearing the yellow dress, the red plaits wound round her head, the jewellery in her ears and on her fingers, Tamara was sitting at her dressing-table staring at an open script.

She looked up and gave a gloomy smile.

'Are you working? Am I disturbing you?' Julie said apologetically. She came quietly into the room and began to change. She tied up her hair, sat down at her dressing-table and began to make up in silence. Julie was happy. She had the odd feeling that, just at this moment, she wouldn't change a single thing about her life – that everything she had was temporarily, beautifully right. The evening's play about to unfold in its magical pattern of wit and sadness, the afternoon gone by with Daniel at her side, the cramped dressing-room with its wilting flowers and shabby old Koala bear, everything was bathed in a kind of soft light.

Tam broke the spell by a sigh.

'What is it, Tam?' Julie said, looking at her companion,

who was noticeably lacking her usual sparkle.

'I don't know. I really don't.'

'Is it your new play? Is it worrying you?'

It was the first time since she'd met Tam that she didn't have a small stab of that despised human emotion, envy. Julie knew she would have needed to be a saint *not* to be a little envious of Tam's good fortune, famous name, position of already established actress, assured future. Julie had struggled with her own envy; she disliked it in herself, and she admired Tam and was fond of her. But this evening the tinge, the twinge, had disappeared.

Tam said, 'No, it isn't the play. I've read it over and over, and of course we haven't started rehearsing, though Dave and I talk about nothing else. I don't know what's rong with me tonight. I have this feeling in my bones. You know those old countrywomen who can tell exactly when it's going to rain because of their rheumatic joints? I'm like that tonight. *I'm* convinced it is going to pour. On me.'

'Cheer up. Maybe John Locking will sweep you off your feet in your love scenes. Perhaps that's what you're afraid of.'

Tam giggled slightly and began to discuss Locking's latest misbehaviour. Could Julie credit it? Locking had suggested to Margery Wylie that Tam should play her best scene *almost hidden behind that damned tree*!

Julie had been looking forward to tonight's performance but when it started, somehow it didn't seem to go well that evening. There was some mysterious ingredient missing. Was it because of today's depressing rain that the audience seemed so uninvolved? Was it the middle of the week – a kind of doldrums? As Julie and Tam came up the stairs at the end of Act One, both of them complained about the audience and agreed that they found tonight's performance depressing. How flattened they felt by such a lack of response.

'It's awful. Flat, flat, flat as a pancake!' Tam said, pushing open the dressing-room door.

'Indeed,' said a voice in a ringing tone.

The girls halted as if frozen in the still of a film.

Seated on the old sofa, long legs elegantly crossed and wearing an expression of irony, was Sir Robert Waring.

'Dad!'

Tam gave a shriek, and forgetting costume, wig and jewels, flew across the room and flung her arms round his neck.

'Careful, child. I don't want make-up on my velvet cuffs,' said Robert Waring, giving his daughter a brief kiss. He looked over at Julie, still standing by the door, and said, 'Tamara. Introduce me.'

Tam unwrapped herself from embracing her father.

'I'm so sorry. Dad took me by surprise, I haven't seen him for *weeks*. Julie, this is my father. Dad, this is Julie Woods, who's playing Hero, by the way.'

'How do you do,' said Sir Robert Waring, coming over to take Julie's hand. He gripped it very hard and Julie's ring practically sawed her finger in half.

She had never seen Robert Waring before 'in real life', only in plays and films. Her determination to disappear quietly if there was any sign of him coming to visit his daughter had failed. Julie gave him a shy smile and wondered desperately if she could think of an excuse to slip out of the dressing-room. She'd never wanted to meet him, he was so much larger than life. Larger than *her* life. Now he stood in the dressing-room, making it smaller, untidier and more claustrophobic than usual, and she thought : I had no idea you were so beautiful.

It was a word still not used often about a man and it was exactly what he was. With his high cheek bones and thick black hair touched with grey, mobile mouth and enormous brilliant eyes, Robert Waring was beautiful. He was also, though he'd scarcely said a word, alarming.

'When did you arrive? Are you going out front to have a look at the play? Have you seen Old Mother Wylie yet?' asked Tam, hanging round her father like a teenage fan.

Robert Waring accepted his daughter's manner to him rather as if some small creature, a budgerigar for instance, had landed on his shoulder.

'I have not "just arrived", Tamara. I saw your first act and I've called to tell you I am here before some member of your company pops in with the news – '

The door of the dressing-room burst open as he was speaking and Chris came in, crying : 'Tam ! Guess what ! Your old man's Rolls – '

Chris caught sight of Sir Robert before he had finished the sentence and stood, much as the girls had done, frozen in the doorway.

'As you say, the old man's Rolls is at the stage door and he *is* here,' said Sir Robert. 'Now buzz off, young man.'

Chris vanished as if through a trap door, and Tam and Julie laughed.

Robert Waring looked pleased. He liked to make people

laugh; it was his favourite pastime.

'Do sit down, both of you,' he said, as the girls stood there in their costumes, looking helpless. 'You have seven minutes before curtain up. Relax. Well, Tamara. Tell me about the rest of the production. Am I going to relish the next act?'

The seven minutes accurately measured by Robert Waring went by in a flash; Tam chattered, Robert Waring commented, Julie said nothing. But Robert Waring looked over at her often and once asked her a question, and when she replied he smiled. It was the smile which made the seven minutes disappear. It was a famous smile and Julie was unaware, until it was turned upon her, just how powerful it was. His bright eyes were like two blue rays, and when he smiled his whole face altered and seemed to swim. It was as if, for a moment, he said something to her without words, something beautiful and important. And in receiving the smile she found herself concentrating intensely, and then at once forgetting what it was that he had conveyed.

He looked at his watch.

'I must get back to my seat. I won't come back in the second interval, I'm meeting Margery Wylie and I'll thank you not to call her by that vulgar nickname, Tamara. I'll see you after the play. Au revoir.'

He turned at the door and said to Tam, 'Speak *up* in the church scene. No mumbling!'

The music for Act II was playing over the intercom; Julie pinned on her wedding veil, Tam picked up her prayer book and silk gloves.

'Imagine Dad appearing!' Tam said, and sighed. 'I knew rain was on the way, didn't I? I tell you, Julie, it's a whole hurricane.'

'I don't understand. Just because your father—'

'He doesn't like my performance,' Tam said, and as she pulled on her gloves Julie saw that her hands were trembling. 'Dad got me the chance to play Beatrice, you know. Old Mother Wylie worships him, like everybody does, that's why she gave it to me. I've always thirsted to play Beatrice, and David was mad for me to do *Much Ado* before his play because there's a bit of the Beatrice character in his girl too. Dad will now tell Old Mother Wylie I'm no good, and what's more he'll tell *me* and I'll be finished for the rest of the run . . .'

Julie had never seen Tam upset before. 'Don't be crazy, Tam! You're good. He thinks you are. He *must*!'

'No, no, I know him!' was the miserable answer as the girls hurried down, and a moment later were engulfed in the play.

It was odd to know Sir Robert Waring was in the house. Despite the dazzle of lights, Julie soon singled out where he was sitting; the shape of his head, a certain style to his shoulders, made him recognizable. She also realized the moment Act II began that the public had discovered who was in the stalls. The quality of the audience was completely altered. It had been flat, but now it bubbled. It had been slow; now it was quick and intuitive. It had been pedestrian; now it got every nuance. The audience's brightness altered the performance, and *Much Ado* began to go wonderfully. And all, thought Julie, because of a certain pair of broad shoulders and two eyes like sunray lamps.

The play ended with the dance, the girls whirled round in their pattern of love and renewed happiness, the audience, proud of itself, roared its applause.

The girls took their curtsies and finally left the stage and went upstairs together.

How was Robert Waring there before them?

He was again seated on the shabby sofa, waving his programme which he had folded into a fan.

'You left before the curtain!' accused Tam, thinking it wise to attack first.

'Don't be absurd, Tamara. I have longer legs than you. And I move faster. Congratulations. Very nice.'

He said this quite kindly while Tam and Julie stood in front of him like schoolgirls at a prize-giving. At their twin expressions he burst out laughing.

'I wish you could see your faces,' he said, straightening his own. 'You don't believe I enjoyed myself, do you?'

'No, we don't,' said Tam flatly. 'I expect you liked Julie – well of course you did – but you thought I was *awful*!'

She was pale and she had begun to tremble again. She lifted her hands and tugged at the long red plaits, one of which fell down and hung over her shoulder like an old skipping rope.

'Leave your hair alone. It suits you. Tidy it up and leave it like that when I take you out to dine, Tamara. And stop fussing. I like your Beatrice. She's a spirited miss. A little gauche at times but there's no harm in that. Too many actresses wait to play her until they're on the wrong side of forty. Of course when you play her for me later on we'll do some more work on your comedy but – '

31

'Dad!'

Tam had thrown her arms round his neck again, and Robert Waring, unloosing her throttling grasp, raised his eyes to heaven and murmured to Julie as if to an old friend: 'So impulsive, isn't she? Gentle heaven, who would think she was a grown woman, and a married one at that!'

Tam, who had caught on to the magic word 'when you play Beatrice for me', was a changed girl. She was bursting with merriment and spirits as she pulled up a chair by her father's side, listened reverently to his comments on the play, agreeing with every word. Julie, the practical one, looked about for the bottle of sherry. She offered a glass to Sir Robert.

'Alas, no,' he said. 'It looks delicious but I am wasting, as the jockeys call it. And Tamara must not drink either or she'll get a trace of that double chin she worries about. But do have a glass, Miss Julie.'

'Oh no. I won't, thank you.'

Her shy manner and hoarse little voice, so unlike Tam's, seemed to amuse him. He gave her another of his bright blue looks. Julie wished he wouldn't. A few more of those, she thought, and she'd have sunstroke.

'I haven't spoken about your Hero yet,' he said. 'It was a clever performance. Delicate and clever. You avoided playing the girl as a ninny. I've seen too many actresses play her like that.'

'Thank you, Sir Robert.'

'A clever performance,' he repeated.

Julie heard, in his actor's resonant voice, just that hint of patronage she'd been expecting. How she wished the beautiful man, so much larger than life, so much too big for her own conception of it, would go!

As if conjured by her thought, he stood up.

'I must leave you girls to get out of your costumes. Tamara, will you dine with me? Good. David telephoned to say he is not coming down this evening, and I told him I would be taking you to the Heron. He will be ringing you there. Now remember; leave those plaits. I like them. I'll pick you up in exactly twenty minutes.'

He came across the small room in a stride and took Julie's hand in his own warm, strong one.

'Good night,' he said. 'And congratulations.'

Tam was changed, made up and ready in less than twenty

minutes; it amused Julie to see her room mate hurry so. Tam usually took her time, murmuring fondly if Julie reminded her of the clock, 'Darling David won't mind. He knows I'm a scatterbrain.'

Tonight the scatterbrain, a changed character, was ready in exactly the time her father had allowed; she came dancing over to say good night to Julie, looking pleased with herself.

'Isn't it super? What he said, I mean. I hope you didn't find him too monstrous, Julie. I know he's a bit of a shock when one first meets him, the old vampire. But he meant what he said about you. You didn't believe him, did you? But he *never* says things unless he means them. It would bore him to pay compliments. If he says you're good,' said Tam simply, 'you *are*.'

She gave Julie a pat on the shoulder and ran out of the room.

The dressing-room was quiet when Tam had gone. In the distance there was a muffled burst of laughter and a moment later Julie heard a group of the actors going by, their voices stronger and fuller than those of ordinary people. Julie pushed on her shoes and glanced over at the old sofa. It was covered in faded green velvet and had a little cushion that she'd brought with her to the dressing-room, a small sign of home. Her mother had made it for her and covered it with apricot silk. The cushion was crushed against the back of the sofa where Robert Waring had leaned against it.

She stood staring down at the old cushion. Suddenly she realized just how silly she must look, mooning over where 'He' had sat like a love-sick Victorian girl. But Julie wasn't love-sick. Her uneasy feelings, disturbed, depressed, yearning even, were only to do with work. 'Only,' thought Julie. 'Only' was scarcely the right word. For to act was to catch a sort of marvellous sickness, a continuous desire as strong as love. She was in love with the theatre, happy when she was playing, in turn sad and hopeful when she was not. And pressed against her mother's cushion, looking at her with piercing eyes, had sat the very Spirit of Theatre, Robert Waring whom every actor in the world called 'Sir'.

Sir had said he liked her performance, hadn't he?

But Julie still didn't believe what Tam had told her. Sir had come round to see his daughter who just happened, in the small matey Sheridan, to share a dressing-room with an unknown girl called Julie Woods. Sir probably felt sorry for Julie. 'I suppose when you're famous you faintly remember what it was like when you'd just begun,' she thought. She tried to recall how and where Sir began his career, to visualize him as a boy at the Vic or as a very young man in Hollywood movies. But she couldn't. She could only remember how he'd looked *here*, half an hour ago.

He was marvellous, of course. She wished she'd never met him.

It had been instinctive in her to hope she could avoid meeting Tam's famous father. Of course Julie was ambitious, she was an actress and took her career seriously. But she was clear-headed and she knew that to be introduced to world-famous people wasn't the way to get oneself a modest job at the start of a career. Julie had known other players who pulled strings, begged favours, got themselves introduced to directors and stars. One of Julie's friends in Rep had managed to go over to Hollywood and get introductions to what she had mockingly termed 'The Old Time Greats'. The same girl, with tales of amazing dinner parties and swimming parties, sneak previews and screen tests, was back in Rep twelve months later. All her adventure had led to had been a dose of San Francisco flu.

Julie took her coat off the hook and said aloud, 'And a dose of Sir Robert Waring flu is what I'm *not* going to catch.'

She walked past the stage door out into the warm night-time street.

The rain was over, the air smelled of lime-tree flowers. The street was empty except for a couple, their arms round each other's shoulders, looking in a furniture shop window. Something about the man's thick hair reminded Julie of Daniel, and she had a pang, a moment's painful stab somewhere in the region of her heart. She remembered Daniel's dark eyes, a certain way of talking, and how she'd dashed into the dressing-room tonight . . . so happy!

Damn Sir Robert Waring. It was true; being connected with the Great did upset you. It made you forget real things, it reduced the size of everything because you measured it beside something vast – a towering talent, for instance.

She'd thought Daniel out of her league; how much, much more was the person who'd just been sitting in her dressing-room.

Much Ado will be over in less than three weeks and I'm sure I shan't see Tam again because that's how it goes, Julie thought philosophically. A little voice inside her asked her if she would see Daniel again. Julie did not answer that voice.

She walked down the road and turned up the narrow side street with its line of thin trees, where she had her digs. There was the old-fashioned brick house behind the black railings; lights shone in the ground floor windows and she thought: 'Good, Chris is home.' She looked forward to sandwiches, hot milk and honey with him, and a long chat about Sir.

As she came towards the house, her thoughts turned wistfully to Daniel again. She stared at the pavement as she walked.

'Miss Julie,' said a voice.

Julie gave a violent start.

There was a low laugh.

Parked outside her lodgings was a huge coffee-and-cream-coloured Rolls-Royce. The car glittered under the lamplight like a chariot of the gods. Parked beside Chris's padlocked bicycle it looked very absurd.

The car window was unwound and Robert Waring was leaning out. Behind him, Julie saw Tam.

'Miss Julie,' repeated Robert Waring, in the voice that was known across the globe.

He beckoned. Julie walked over to the car.

'Why not come and dine with us?' said Robert Waring.

2

Julie slept deeply for what seemed the whole night. She woke, convinced it was time to get up. But it was dark and when she switched on her bedside light it was only quarter to five.

She lay back and closed her eyes, hoping for gentle sleep again. But she was broad awake. Julie went over in her mind the whole extraordinary evening gone by, from the moment she'd seen the huge car glittering at the front door of her digs, and a ringing voice had said: 'Come and dine with us.'

Both Sir and Tam had welcomed her warmly as she climbed into the car. Tam was in high spirits.

'Dad's ordered a special supper at the Heron. And guess what? We're having it in a private room because he says the hotel audience have seen quite enough of him for the present.'

It was only five hours ago that Julie and Tam had been with Sir in a small Tudor room, eating supper by candlelight. She remembered how Sir had made them laugh helplessly; she remembered how fascinating his conversation had been. But what exactly had he said? It was annoying that now she tried earnestly to remember, she couldn't recall a word. Only the expressions of that infinitely expressive face.

She sighed as she glanced at her watch and saw that only half an hour had crawled by. She got out of bed to pull back the curtains; it was a relief to see that day *was* coming, there was a pale ghostly light in the sky, and the trees of a garden opposite were beginning to stand out from the dark. Julie climbed back into bed, gave her pillows a punch, and went on thinking about last night.

One thing she did remember, very clearly, was her own thoughts when she'd walked home from the Sheridan just before she saw Robert Waring's car. She had been thinking then that the company of the Great was bad for people; it took away a sense of proportion. And she had been pro-phetically right, for already meeting Sir had the peculiar effect of blurring other things. For instance, the time she'd spent with Daniel now seemed rather far away and dim. She didn't want that to happen; she told herself that it was Daniel, and not the star, who mattered to her.

And yet, thought Julie, sighing, how did she know that was true either? Everything that had happened to her in the last few days was rather unreal. Perhaps she and Daniel weren't destined to be close friends, any more than she and Tam. When *Much Ado* closed, a lot of other things would close too, such as her relationship with Tam and David, and that extraordinary chance of meeting Sir Robert Waring. And per-haps she wouldn't see Daniel any more, when their sharing of mutual friends was gone. That was what happened during the run of a play; you made friends and had a kind of life connected with it. But when the play ended, and your per-formance was over and forgotten, everything else seemed to disappear too.

Julie lay uneasily, trying to get what she often called in her mind 'down to earth'. She knew it was easy to be hurt in the magical dangerous world of the theatre; she was cautious. She knew that when things seemed exciting and promising, she mustn't drop her guard.

Julie's determination to take things cautiously, testing them step by step for the possibility of disappointment, had always been part of her nature.

Her father had laughed at her when she was a child. 'Aren't you looking forward to the party, Julie? All the other kids are.'

'No, Dads. Not really. In case it's not as lovely as they say.'

'You are an old-fashioned little thing. Looking forward is half the fun,' he had said, looking down from his tall, thin height to the solemn child in front of him.

It was too early to go downstairs in search of breakfast, so Julie sat down by the open window and picked up the script of David Bryden's new play. David had lent it to her yesterday.

The early sunlight flooding through the window warmed her bare arms. She was reading absorbedly when she thought she heard somebody call her name. She glanced round, thinking it must be Chris. But the door remained closed.

'Julie!'

There it was again. Surely it was coming from the garden. She looked down from the window. A man was standing, arms folded, beside a magnificent bush covered with crimson roses. He was dressed in a black velvet suit and a white silk shirt as sparkling as the day itself.

It was Sir.

'Julie!' he called, lowering his voice and glancing towards the house.

Wondering what on earth this vision could want, she leaned out and waved.

'Hallo,' she called softly. 'Can I help?'

She vaguely imagined he wanted something to do with Tam.

'Yes, you can,' replied Sir Robert in a whisper that practically carried to London. 'You can come and have breakfast. Breakfast!' He mimed drinking from a cup and buttering some bread. 'Have you had any?'

'No,' hissed Julie, still hanging from the window.

'Good! Come on down.'

Where was caution now? She snatched up her handbag and ran down the stairs two at a time.

As she came flying out of the door, Robert Waring had his face buried in the roses. When he saw her, he broke off the largest flower and presented it to her, saying: 'For you.'

'Oh. Thank you very much. My landlady will have a pink fit,' said Julie, taking the huge, rain-wet bloom.

37

'Then I advise you to take it to the theatre and put it in a vase. Come along. Breakfast is ready.'

He shepherded her down the garden and through the gate to where the Rolls was parked. The engine was already purring, and the moment they had got into the car the chauffeur started off.

They seemed quite *certain* I'd come, thought Julie. It's like a getaway car in a Mafia-type movie.

The car window was open and a soft breeze fanned her cheeks. Her companion said, glancing at her approvingly: 'It's nice of you to come and have breakfast with me.'

'It's nice of you to ask me,' said Julie primly.

'It isn't "nice" at all,' Robert Waring remarked. 'I want to talk to you without my daughter buzzing around like a mosquito.'

Julie was amused to hear Sir repeating exactly what Daniel had said, about wanting to see her without Tam. She couldn't help smiling and was answered by a grin from Sir.

In the brilliant sunlight, the clever beautiful face was lined. She thought how plastic a true actor's face became, marked by humour and by tragedy, by a kind of mockery, by wariness. His forehead had deep creases from a habit of raising his brow when he laughed. His mouth, in repose, was determined; hard, almost. With high cheek bones and long eyes, and a look of shrewdness and power, he could have been some wily Red Indian chief.

'Great luck I caught you before breakfast,' he said in a lively voice. '*And* by the window. I thought I was going to have to fascinate your landlady. I used to be a dab hand at that. You get up early, Julie. I like an actor who rises with the lark. Rare.'

'I was up particularly early this morning.'

'Well, of course,' he said, in a tone that meant as clearly as if he'd said it. 'That's because you were thinking about me.'

Julie was rather flustered by this, and was relieved when the car turned silently into the long driveway of the Heron Hotel and stopped by the front door.   '

In the entrance hall they were received by the manager. It was the same welcome they had been given the previous evening; Julie supposed Sir was used to creating a buzz of activity wherever he went. He took it as if it was the most natural thing in the world to have the manager bowing low and waving instructions to two waiters, giving an impres-

38

sion of concentrated service. One could just imagine, thought Julie, following the manager up the staircase, that there were literally teams of waiters, chefs, porters, receptionists, hovering to do Sir's slightest wish. Disgraceful, thought Julie, enjoying it.

'Is breakfast ready, Nigel?' enquired Sir Robert, in a hearty man-to-man voice to the manager. 'Some delicious Heron coffee? And rolls?'

'On the table, your Lordship,' said the manager reverently.

The Heron had once been a little Tudor mansion, and its rooms were intimate, almost poky. Julie and Sir were ushered by the manager into the room where they had dined last night. There had been candles then and this morning the sunlight slanted through latticed windows, but the impression of a small, rather secret room remained. One looked for an arras.

When the manager had settled them at the table, and coffee had been poured, and warm rolls and bitter marmalade served, they were left alone. Sir Robert looked over at Julie and gave a huge wink.

'Isn't Nigel superb?' he said, buttering a roll. 'I've known him for years. He used to manage a little place in Covent Garden when I was a young man. I took girls to supper there because it was cheap, but much more because Nigel amused us so much.'

During breakfast Sir was in excellent spirits. He told her stories and when he talked of famous people he altered his face and manner, used their voices so uncannily that Julie felt she was breakfasting with *them*. He said he was going to make a new film very soon.

'I'll be on location in Spain but not for long, fortunately. That's because I play a small part.'

'That's impossible! How could you play a *small* part?'

She was genuinely shocked.

'Perhaps because they're paying me a *small* fortune.'

'That can't be the reason!' She had been with him for an hour and her self-consciousness was quite gone. She said with high contempt, 'As if you would work for *money*!'

It was the first time Julie had seen Robert Waring really laugh. He just lay back in his chair and roared.

'Oh, that's lovely. You're lovely. My dear delicious girl, I always need money. A great deal of money. It is money which buys me the most desirable of all commodities for sale . . . this.' He tapped his wristwatch and then, with an expressive gesture, gripped it with his right hand. 'Time,' he said. 'Time.'

Julie was rather offended by the loud mirth; she was determined to stick to her point since she felt herself misjudged and made to look a simpleton. She repeated stiffly that in her opinion a great actor shouldn't play small parts.

'Why not?' he asked, straightening his face, although his eyes still sparkled.

'Because it's out of balance. Like – like having a blazing fire which only warms a small corner of some huge room, leaving everywhere else dark and chilly. All the people in the room would squash into the corner and the rest of the room would be wasted. Who'd look at the rest of the film or enjoy it if *you* started blazing away in one small bit?'

He did not answer her, but looked at her reflectively. She had no idea what he was thinking; his face, usually so expressive, was enigmatic. His thoughts absorbed him and Julie returned to a cup of lukewarm coffee, thinking : Why did he ask me here? He thinks me naive. So I am. And he doesn't even like me much.'

'I didn't describe the part quite accurately,' he said after a moment. 'It is certainly short; the actual number of lines I speak is quite few. However, I shouldn't have said the part was small. I come in at the end of the picture and tie up one or two things. Most of them, now I come to think of it.'

'You mean you come in and steal it?'

'Oh, I wouldn't go as far as that.'

They finished their meal and he suggested they should go for a walk in the garden.

The lawns that surrounded the hotel were damp but the morning – it was after ten o'clock – was gentle and warm. The gardens were elaborate, criss-crossed with hedges, walks, unexpected sundials and shrubberies. In the distance Julie saw a small lake. There was one grassy walk which ran beside a hedge of enormous rhododendrons; the trees, knitted as close as a solid dark green wall, were nine feet high. Sir Robert led Julie towards this walk and they paced up and down beside the hedges which were covered with lance-shaped buds showing slivers of purple.

'I'm coming to see *Much Ado* again this afternoon,' he remarked casually.

Julie, impressed, said she supposed he was interested in Tam's Beatrice.

'Maybe. She isn't bad, is she?'

40

'*I* think she's lovely.'

He looked amused at her warm praise.

'What has become of your actress's natural jealousy, Miss Woods?'

'Perhaps I haven't any.'

'Fiddle. All actresses have it. I would find it most worrying if they were not constantly competing with each other. How would they progress if we had nothing but sweetness and mutual admiration between them? Very tiresome that would be.'

'Well, I admire Tam and I am not jealous of her. She'll make you a gorgeous Beatrice.'

'She'll have to be five years older,' he said. 'However, I am not sitting through Margery Wylie's not-very-brilliant production this afternoon from father love, you know.'

They had arrived at the end of the rhododendron hedge for the fourth time. Julie wondered if they might perhaps alter course and make towards the lake. She also wondered what Sir Robert meant by not coming to see *Much Ado* on Tam's account. A lot of his remarks required answers she was too mystified to give.

'I suppose you'd like to walk round the lake,' he said accusingly. Julie found herself replying meekly : 'Of course not.'

'Good. It's much better here. About turn.'

Obediently she accompanied him back along the same stretch of lawn; he was striding and she had to trot to keep up with him. He hummed a little tune and then gave an exaggerated sigh very like Tam's. *Some* remark was clearly expected.

'Is anything the matter, Sir Robert?' enquired Julie.

'You didn't seem very interested to learn that I am watching *Much Ado* for the second time in twenty-four hours.'

'Of course I am ! It's wonderful. The audience will be – '

'Damn the audience,' he said disloyally. 'We are talking about you.'

There was a startled pause. Sir Robert stopped walking and looked down at her. Julie, her mouth slightly open, looked back.

'Are we?'

Satisfied at her discomfiture, he began to walk briskly again. 'Yes, we are. I want to see your Hero again. Take another look at you. You're a clever girl, though an inexperienced one.'

You couldn't, thought Julie, thank Sir Robert Waring for

something like that. And anyway if she did he'd only make fun of her.

She wasn't looking forward to seeing Tam when she arrived for the matinée at the Sheridan. She felt positively guilty about her unexpected morning with Tam's father.

She was sitting at her mirror busy with her make-up when Tam burst in, wearing palest green and a mischievous expression.

'Sly boots!' cried Tam, before Julie could utter a word. 'Breakfast with Sir, I hear. What are *you* up to?'

'Surely you can't think –' began Julie, and was answered by a hoot of laughter.

'I'll quote Dad at you,' said Tam. 'And say that if you call yourself an actress and you are *not* up to something, you jolly well should be.'

Tam pulled on her dressing-gown, slapped some cream on her forehead and went on talking. 'Dad rang to say he was coming to the matinée this afternoon – imagine twice! – and would I give a performance "worth seeing" as he rudely put it. He then said he'd breakfasted with you and enjoyed himself. Well, of course,' said Tam, busy with a thick eye-pencil, 'I was bursting to hear about the breakfast but he does so like creating the effect and leaving one hanging in mid-air. Damn. This thing's blunt. So he rang off before I could get another word out of him. What actually happened?'

Julie said it had been very nice and nothing had happened. They'd walked round the garden.

Tam was not satisfied. She wound her red plaits deftly round her head and swallowed a few vitamin pills, plying Julie with teasing questions. *Why* did Julie suppose Sir had appeared again? Hadn't Julie some *theory*? Hadn't Sir given a hint? Had they discussed Sir's Royalty plans? Films?

'No, no, no,' said Julie, laughing. 'Couldn't he just have come over on impulse? I mean, he was a bit bored and we did have fun last night, and he thought "I'll give the little Woods girl some breakfast. That'll knock her out."' Julie made a passable stab at the famous Waring voice.

Tam was dismissive.

'My father never did an impulsive thing in his life. He does everything on *purpose*. I tell you, Julie, he had his reasons for fishing you out of your digs this morning. *I* think he's going to offer you a part ...'

'Don't be ridiculous!' snapped Julie. Disturbed from her

cocoon of caution, she was irritable.

The play began and Julie was glad to be claimed by it. She took on Hero's feelings with relief and love. It was true she was conscious of Sir in the stalls again and that this afternoon's audience had seen him, too. Like last night's audience, they promptly became clever and quick, doing themselves credit. Every laugh rippled. When the play ended and the applause died down, Tam and Julie left the stage feeling inspirited. They expected Sir to join them in their dressing-room, and within a moment or two heard his light, fast step.

He came in wearing an elegant suit of dark silk and a black satin tie. He looked very much the great star, the great name, this afternoon. This wasn't Julie's preposterous companion of the breakfast table who'd crunched hot rolls and made jokes and dragged her up and down the rhododendron walk.

'Margery has asked us to tea in her office,' he remarked after Tam had kissed him, and he'd nodded kindly at Julie who promptly felt he'd turned her right back into a mouse.

'I hope you feel honoured, Tamara,' he said.

'Old Mother Wy – sorry, *Miss* Wylie doesn't like me, Dad. Must I come?'

'Most certainly you must. I have seen her Sheridan plans for the next twelve months and they're good.'

Tam raised her eyebrows and began to undo Beatrice's jewellery, dropping earrings and bracelets on the dressing-table with a heavy chink. Robert Waring turned to Julie.

'Before we go to Margery Wylie's office, I have a small request to make, Julie. Would you like to come and stay the week-end with my sister and myself?'

Startled, Tam turned round with her necklace hanging; Julie blushed scarlet.

Robert Waring went on : 'I thought I might drive down and collect you tomorrow night after the performance. We can be back in London in an hour and a half. You can stay the night in Hampstead and come back here on Sunday evening if that would suit. I can drive you, or Dixon will be glad to if I have work to do. Well? Would you like that? I have a very pretty house, haven't I, Tamara? And don't tell me, Julie,' he added, holding up his hand, palm outwards, 'that it is kind of me. You keep on making these girlish speeches and they're quite unnecessary. You'd make me happy if you would accept, so please say yes.'

'I'd love to,' said Julie.

She looked small and comic in Hero's satin finery and fair curling wig, standing there blushing to her ears. Sir Robert appeared not to notice her embarrassment.

'That's settled then. I'll see you when the curtain comes down tomorrow night. We'll spend Sunday together. You'll like my sister Harriet. She isn't in the least like me!'

Julie was glad to leave the Sheridan after the Wylie tea party. She thanked Sir Robert, avoiding Tam's teasing eye, and walked back to her digs as fast as she could.

It was still warm and bright as it had been this morning when she'd seen Sir Robert standing in her garden. When she arrived at her digs she noted, with guilty amusement, the torn stem where he'd picked her the finest rose on the bush.

Chris was in the hall telephoning and when he saw her he said, 'Hooray. I'll come and call. Good news!'

Julie went to her room, kicked off her shoes and collapsed on to the bed. It seemed ten years since breakfast.

There was a tap on the door.

'Can I come in? Good,' said Chris, who always sounded surprised when he was invited in, immediately after he'd suggested it himself.

He bounded into the room and pulled up the wicker chair. He gave his optimistic smile. He was wearing a yellow T shirt, jeans, leather sandals and no socks. After Sir Robert in his silk suit, Chris looked fourteen.

'That was the Chichester guy on the phone and he says he'll see both of us; as a matter of fact he's coming to see *Much Ado* next week. Good, isn't it?'

'Super. Thank you *very* much, Chris.'

'Oh, it's nothing. I told you your good notices would help me as well,' said Chris, with his usual honesty.

For one glorious minute Julie felt back to normal. There was Chris sitting in the old wicker chair and behind him the familiar shape of a poplar tree, and there was her alarm clock on the bedside table, loudly ticking and reminding her that she had an hour before the evening performance. Chris would now launch into a new tale about the bird in the box office, and that would be familiar too and she'd enjoy it. But Chris leaned forward, arms to knees, and said succinctly: 'Come on. Tell me the whole amazin' tale!'

There was no point in asking what he meant.

'You mean Sir?'

'I mean actually *breakfasting* with the Deity. A man I

44

know who's doing temporary waiting at the Heron said you had two pots of coffee. And Norman at the stage door informed us all . . . Julie you've got us riveted . . . that Sir *asked you to London for the week-end.*'

To Julie's relief, Chris wasn't awestruck or even jealous. He was genuinely amused and waited for the news like a small boy for a handful of Smarties. That was Chris's strength; he never took anything seriously.

She told him the story, beginning with dinner last night and finishing with the invitation for the week-end.

'It isn't a week-end really. I'm going up tomorrow night after the performance, spending Sunday with them and being driven back – get that! – on Sunday night. Sir is *not* driving back with me, I'm glad to say, so I can doze in the back of that huge car and try to get back to normal.'

'Why should you do that, you old prude?'

'Chris!' said Julie, putting out her hand for a piece of the chocolate he was munching, 'I *must* get back to normal. Sir *is* fascinating, one might even say alluring. Right. But he's the big time and I'm the mouse so I'd just better nip quietly back in the wainscot.'

'You might bring us both a lump of cheese while you're about it,' suggested Chris.

They finished the chocolate and continued to chat. Chris suddenly saw the clock and shouted, as usual, 'Hey, Mate! Old Mother Wylie will shoot me!' and rushed off to the theatre. Julie walked sedately back to the Sheridan, changed and made up, feeling back to normal at last. Tam's manner was a help, for Tam seemed to have decided not to tease Julie after all. Julie wondered if Tam's father was at the back of this unaccustomed lenience. All Tam said was: '*What about you!*' and then changed the conversation to talk about David.

During the second interval, when the girls were sitting in their dressing-room having glasses of Russian tea (Tam's new passion), Chris popped his head round the door to announce 'Telephone, Julie!'

Julie followed Chris down the corridor which ran beside the dressing-rooms.

She picked up the telephone, trying to speak against a background of chat from the next-door dressing-rooms.

'Julie?' said an attractive voice. 'It's Daniel. I've done a great swathe of work today and it's looking in good shape. Can we meet tomorrow? What about lunch? The weather

45

forecast is good; I thought we'd take a picnic.'
'I'd love that! Shall I get the food?'
She was so pleased that her voice was quite hoarse.
'Will you? That'll be great. I'll bring the wine. I can be down earlyish. When would suit you?'
They discussed the time, and as they were talking, Julie saw John Locking passing by, wearing his green and gold costume as Benedick. Locking made a friendly face at Julie, and she thought : You're the level of actor I *understand*. He seemed positively cosy after Sir.
'Julie?' said Daniel. 'Are you still there?'
'Yes. I'm here.'
'You don't sound your happy self.'
'Oh I am. I am now you've rung,' she said and he laughed.

Julie might make a joke of it with Chris, or touch on it lightly with Tam, but she was not looking forward to the coming week-end with Robert Waring. It was a marvellous relief that before the ordeal started she was to spend some time with Daniel.

Now that Robert Waring had disappeared back to London and she was out of his magnetic field, Julie felt her heart sink at the thought of going to his house; if she could have got out of the invitation she would have done. She simply didn't enjoy being with a man as famous as that; it might put one on one's mettle but it wasn't any fun. She wasn't good at it. She had just managed to enjoy having Tam Waring and David as friends, although both were well-known in the theatre. But they at least were still *young*. And as for Daniel he wasn't famous at all though his work was admired by pros. You could, thought Julie, be friends with Daniel as an equal even if he was rather rich compared with Chris and herself. But as an acquaintance – as a friend – Robert Waring was out of the question.

How could you cope with anybody so famous? How could there be a conversation worth having? He wouldn't listen, anyway. When you were with a great big thumping star, you became a cipher. Julie was 22, conscious of her inexperience, ambitious and shy by turn. Being with Robert Waring made things ridiculously uneven; one side of the scale so high, the other so low. What could you make out of that?

Why do I want to make anything? scoffed Julie to herself. He's like Tam. A temporary happening. He came to the Sheridan by chance because his daughter was playing there

46

and he met me by chance, because she and I shared a dress-ing-room! I shall go and spend this dire week-end with the Warings, and when it's over I dare say I'll fascinate Chris and my family with first-hand Tales of the Great. And that'll be that.

On Saturday morning Julie had a sociable breakfast with her landlady, Mrs White, in the kitchen. Then she went out shopping in the sunshine, bought food for the picnic, and was swinging home with a loaded basket when she saw Daniel's car at the gate. It was a very different sight from Robert Waring's chariot of the gods; Daniel's car had the hood down, it looked as open as a yacht. Daniel was sitting at the wheel, the sun lighting his curly dark hair and sallow face.

'Good morning, Daniel,' she said, leaning over the car.

'The lovely Julie.'

He looked up and just for a second they almost kissed. But the moment passed. They discussed the picnic and Daniel fished out an ordnance survey map, the same map on which he had discovered the Roman villa.

'Come and sit next to me and take a look at our route. We'll follow this little winding road there, and drive down here, and that B road and there's the wood. Look. There. And the river goes right through it. What do you think? Does that look an interesting drive?'

'Gorgeous.'

They drove out of the town in the bright sunshine. It was pleasantly early and as they passed a church with a blue clock in its tower, Daniel murmured, 'We've got three hours.'

The car slipped through villages and down steep leafy lanes which Daniel appeared to recognize. He said with satisfaction, 'That's right. There's the monument.'

'What monument?'

'The one on the map, you fool!'

The road turned a corner and began to run alongside a small river edged with trees. 'It's the same river we had supper by at David's Spanish place,' Daniel said. 'Only that's about ten miles away. Look, there's my wood at the top of that field.'

They parked the car on a broad grass verge, Julie took her basket and Daniel his bottle of wine. They set off through a gate and up a steep meadow thick with marguerites. They talked eagerly; there seemed such a lot to say, about the sunny weather, the wine Daniel had brought, his work, the full houses at the Sheridan, David Bryden's play. But Julie did

47

not say a word about Robert Waring.

Still talking, they reached the edge of the little copse. It was a wood of young hazels, tall slender trees with narrow trunks and tapering branches. The yellowish-green leaves threw a dappled shade on the ground which was covered in young bracken. Daniel led the way through the undergrowth, picking at brambles and branches to keep them out of the way.

'There's the river. And a bank straight from *Midsummer Night's Dream*,' announced Daniel.

He spread a rug on the mossy ground under a hazel tree. Nearby was the small fast-flowing river, winding its way through the wood, the water dark brown from last year's leaves, twiggy, fresh-smelling, sparkling with gleams of sunshine.

Julie sat beside him, and they unpacked the picnic: cold chicken, a long cos lettuce, peaches, french bread and a hunk of unsalted butter, a punnet of shiny strawberries.

'Oh! I forgot the knife!'

'How's this?' said Daniel, flourishing a pocket knife which was also a corkscrew. 'I never travel without it.'

They ate, lying on their elbows in the dappled shade of the lanky hazels. They drank white wine from paper cups and Daniel looked lazily at the wild flowers growing beside them. There were forget-me-nots at the river's edge, and nearby was a little patch of frail-stemmed anemones.

'I love wild flowers,' Daniel said. 'I use them in designs sometimes. They mean more than cultivated flowers. They are not self-conscious.'

'Daniel, how can you say flowers are self-conscious? What about the perfectly ordinary roses in Mrs White's garden? All they do is flower away obligingly and mind their own business,' said Julie, laughing.

And then she remembered an expressive hand picking one of those roses; it had not seemed a 'perfectly ordinary' flower then. It was still in her dressing-room.

Daniel didn't notice a shade of embarrassment cross her face. He was lying full length, his long legs stretched on the twig-strewn ground. He said ruminatively, 'Why does food taste so good in the open air? This peach. And the bread. I feel like Mole in *Wind in the Willows*. "I don't know when I've tasted better." Maybe it's the company I keep; do you suppose that's why the food tastes so good?' he said, rolling over on one elbow and looking at her.

Just then, Julie felt again a sudden inexplicable happiness, the same feeling she'd had before with Daniel. It flooded through her like the river nearby, sparkling and swirling. It enhanced everything . . . the forget-me-nots with their juicy stalks, the rich-coloured water, the pattern of hazel leaves, the taste of the wine, the sound of birds. The wood was changed and became, as Daniel had said, a place where magic things could happen. And Daniel himself lying near her, big, relaxed, with his attractive sallow face and mouth which turned up at the corners, deep lazy voice, strong, kindly personality, Daniel was changed too. More familiar. Dearer.

'You've gone quiet, Julie,' he remarked. 'You're a bit of a dreamy girl, aren't you? A thoughtful girl. You like to ponder. Imagine somebody beautiful *and* quiet. Sensational.'

'You mean women talk too much.'

'Women? Lord, no. I mean people talk too much. I do. David Bryden does. Tam does. Clover does.'

'Who's Clover?' asked Juliet, rather too quickly.

He burst out laughing.

'You sound quite put out. I like that,' he said. 'How flattering. Clover, dear Julie, is the girl who works at the studio with me. Clover Stornaway. She and I have worked together for years.'

'Is she nice?' enquired Julie, hoping her voice sounded casual.

'A dear girl. Earnest. Dedicated. She has huge owl-like glasses and a passion for the theatre which is a bit exhausting. I found her originally painting scenery at a Rep in Sussex; she was all splashed with white paint like a comedian in a silent movie. She looked sweet. I took a fancy to her and we talked a bit (well, Clover talked and I listened) and we had a drink and the long and the short of it was I offered her a job.'

'I suppose she must be clever,' said Julie, feeling slightly better about Clover.

'Not very. She's devoted, mad about the job, works every week-end and spends days in the V and A on top of ladders. She knows every source book and every designer and actor in London and rings me up at breakfast-time to talk shop; also at one in the morning. Sometimes I wish Clover wasn't quite so dedicated. Makes me feel guilty. She ought to have a man around.'

'Hasn't she?'

'Now and again but it never lasts. She quarrels with him

or bosses him about (she's a bossy character) and then he goes and Clover's busy with our next production, which, strangely enough, she seems to prefer. You'll like her. She's a dear. Tell you what,' said Daniel, chewing a piece of grass, 'why don't I come down and fetch you on Sunday and drive you back to London? You could see our studio and we could lunch somewhere and I'll introduce you to Clover and you can see the new Bryden designs. Would that appeal?'

While Daniel was speaking, delighted at the prospect of spending Sunday with her, Julie had been getting steadily more and more uncomfortable. A number of times during lunch she'd thought of telling him about Sir, including the week-end invitation. But during the last hour, Daniel and she had been so happy that Julie had pushed away the thought of mentioning Sir. She'd just concentrated on Daniel.

Now she wished she'd followed her instinct.

When he finished speaking she said, 'I'd *love* to come with you, Daniel. Please ask me again. But the fact is that this Sunday – '

She told him lamely about Sir's invitation.

Daniel raised his eyebrows and said nothing.

Julie felt impelled to add, 'I don't want to go, as a matter of fact.'

He still didn't speak and suddenly she was nervous. Surely Daniel couldn't think . . . what couldn't he think?

'Daniel.'

'Yes?'

'Now it's you who's gone quiet.'

'I was thinking Robert Waring is nobody's fool.'

'What does that mean?'

'It means that you interest him – as a girl – as an actress – probably both. He certainly moves fast.'

Julie heard herself giving the sort of exaggerated sigh that Tam and Sir used. She said, 'It isn't like that at all! He's a quirky man, a spoiled one. He's rich and both daughters are married and I suppose he gets bored sometimes. It's obvious he bores easily. I'm just a whim from the local Rep. So the whim gets asked up for the week-end. That's all it is. Thank heaven!'

Daniel sat up and poured himself another cup of wine in silence. He lifted the bottle to offer her some, but she shook her head, waiting for him to speak. She was uncomfortable.

'I wonder,' he said finally.

'What do you wonder?'

50

'If you're quite as unworldly as you make out.'

'I don't understand you.' She felt depressed and chilled. The sun had gone behind a cloud, the little river looked gloomy, swirling by like time itself. All the deckled pattern had gone from the twig-strewn ground.

'Surely it occurs even to you, Julie,' he said with faint but recognizable sarcasm, 'that an introduction to Robert Waring is a prize. A great big prize. One that actresses give their eye teeth for. What are *you* going to do with that great big prize? You told me the other day you were worried about being out of work.'

Suddenly Julie was angry at being misjudged, and at the cold tone he used to her. She said sharply, 'If you want to believe I'm fainting with delight at the prospect of staying with him, all right, believe that too. The fact is, and I don't care if you believe it or not, I *don't enjoy* being with anybody as famous as that. I'm simply not a human being when he's around. He stalks about like a – like a great cat – throwing those huge eyes to heaven or being so funny that I collapse with laughter, of *course*,which is what he wants because I'm the audience. An audience of one. I do *not* want to be rushed off in a Rolls, feeling stupid, or made to stay in a strange expensive house and meet Sir's sister (whom Tam may love but I think will terrify the life out of me). As I say,' continued Julie, her voice sharper still, '*I do not want to go* and I'm dreading it. I don't like the rôle of handmaiden to the Great. And if *you* get it in for me because of Sir I shall cry!'

'My dear girl!'

He leaned forward, took her in his arms and kissed her.

They lay back under the hazel trees, pressed close. They kissed for a long, long time. When she opened her eyes, she was conscious of the sunlight again, of the deckled light, of Daniel's lovely face, of his mouth pressed again on hers.

'Oh Daniel.'

He kissed her, called her gentle names, murmured, pushed his face against her hair. Suddenly, still with his arms round her, he looked at his watch and gave a shout of horror.

'We've got twenty minutes to get you back to the theatre!'

The idyll broke as if they'd smashed a looking-glass.

They sprang to their feet like people in a fire. Picnic things were thrown into the basket, the rug snatched up, and they began to run through the wood like wild things, Daniel stretching back his arm to pull Julie at his faster pace. They arrived panting, fell into the car and drove off with the engine roaring. It was only Daniel's fast car and the fact that he knew the way through traffic-free lanes that brought Julie, trembling, to the stage door in time.

As she scrambled out, he called, 'Goodbye, angel. I'll telephone you at Sir's tomorrow at six. We'll spend the evening together. Promise?'

'Oh yes. I promise.'

They exchanged a brief passionate kiss and Julie rushed helter-skelter into the stage door.

To Julie's relief, Sir Robert did not come to the dressing-room after the evening performance to collect her. She had already changed into a new white trouser suit and was waiting when Norman, at the stage door, rang through.

'Norman says His Lordship is waiting in the car,' announced Tam who had answered the telephone. 'It sounds like a Lonsdale comedy.'

She went over to Julie and gave her a warm kiss.

'Wish me luck,' Julie said.

'You won't need it, darlin',' said Tam. 'Don't be nervous. He's lovely really. And his bark's much worse than his bite.'

'But he even frightens you.'

Tam giggled and said Julie looked exactly like a martyr off to the stake.

'He'll be gentle as a dove, I promise. He's got a *very* soft heart, you'll be staggered at how sweet he can be. And my Aunty Harriet is a darling, she'll look after you like mad. You'll have a super time in Hampstead. I always do!'

Julie laughed, thinking inevitably: But I am not Sir's daughter'. Taking a deep breath, she walked down the corridor and the stairs to the stage door. A group of actors passed by; Julie wondered if she imagined that they all looked at her coldly. Nobody spoke to her. She supposed they'd heard the news! actors knew everything.

When she saw the coffee-and-cream car by the stage door she had a moment of sheer panic and it was only because it needed more nerve to run than to stay that Julie managed to cross the pavement. The door of the car flew open as she approached, and Sir leaned forward to take her hand.

'We'll be back in Hampstead in an hour and a half,' Robert Waring said. 'Is it unkind of me to rush you home instead of giving you dinner first?'

'Oh no. I'm not a bit hungry. Often, after a performance, I

can only manage bread and milk,' Julie said.

'Yes, I know that feeling. Playing can take the appetite away. Yet at other times an actor falls on food like a wolf,' Robert Waring murmured.

He switched on the car radio and they drove back to London to music. They talked about *Much Ado*, and he told her how once in New York when he'd been playing Benedick, the actress playing Beatrice opposite him had tumbled into the orchestra pit.

'One minute we were having a duel of wits and the next she vanished like the Demon King.'

'Was she hurt?'

'What a soft heart you have!' he said sardonically. 'No, she was not. But my speech was.'

Shop made the time fly, and quite soon the car had reached London and they were driving through bright, busy streets, and then climbing towards Hampstead. The car turned into a quiet, hilly road edged with chestnut trees and slowed down.

Julie looked out curiously. The large house at the top of the hill was set back from the road, partly hidden by high old-fashioned hedges which reminded Julie of the rhododendron hedge at the hotel. Apparently Robert Waring liked hedges! The chauffeur opened the car door, and then took out Julie's miniature suitcase from the boot as if he were unpacking the luggage of an ambassador.

Robert Waring walked with Julie up the flagged path to the house, which shone with lights. Before he could put his key into the latch, the door opened. A small woman came out, and he put his arms round her and embraced her.

'Harry!' he exclaimed, as if he had not seen her for months. 'This is Julie Woods, Tam's friend. Julie, meet my sister.'

Julie shook hands shyly. Harriet Waring was not in the least the sort of person she'd imagined. In Julie's mind anybody with the name Waring was autocratic and high-spirited, sparkling, actorish. This little lady had a fine worn face and hair cut in a medieval bob like a middle-aged troubadour. She had the unmistakable walk of somebody who'd been a ballet dancer, and she wore flat satin slippers which were almost ballet shoes. She was dressed in dark grey, and her face, in which there was a faint reflection of her brother's, was haggard and refined by age. It had distinction and kindness.

'I'm so glad to meet you, Julie. Tam talks about you all

53

the time. Do come in. You must be tired after giving a performance and a long drive too. Supper is ready.'

'Has anybody rung, Harry?' asked Robert Waring, taking Julie's jacket and somehow welcoming her into the house without saying anything specific. Julie was warmed by his manner and by Harriet's; both of them had an extraordinary hospitality.

'Seven people rang. I've made a list. Someone rang from America in a bit of a state but Bernard is coping with him. Periandra rang three times.'

Robert Waring groaned and Harriet said in a matter-of-fact voice, 'It's all right. The telephone's switched off.'

She led the way through a spacious hallway, past a curving staircase and a grandfather clock, into the drawing-room.

'I laid supper here so that you can sit on the settee, it's more comfortable when one is tired. I'll light the candles and leave you,' Harriet said.

Julie looked round one of the most beautiful rooms she'd ever seen. It was a great spacious place, with a grand piano and pale embroidered carpets; it was crowded with the variety of objects that famous people are given by those who love or admire them . . . a huge scarlet vase with a dragon on it, a silver rapier, a marble bust, a painted figure of Othello, a set of bells from Kashmir, and everywhere drawings, paintings, engravings and photographs. It was a room as full of the theatre as the heart could wish and it was curious to see portraits of Robert Waring everywhere, as Hamlet, as Eugene Onegin, as Romeo, as Brutus. They stared down from the walls, and when Julie looked round she saw more of these, in photographs, drawings, miniatures.

'I know, I know,' he said. 'I must apologize for my face all over the place. It's like being haunted, isn't it? I'll get rid of them one of these days.'

Harriet caught Julie's eye just then, and Julie thought she discerned a faint concealed grin.

There was a table laid by the settee, covered with lace and dishes of cold food. Harriet lit the candles which were set in a bowl of garnet roses.

'I'll say good night,' she said. 'Sir will show you to your room, Julie. It's overlooking the garden and quiet. You have a nice bathroom – Tam's favourite. It's peacock blue.'

'Must you go, Harry? Stay and chat,' said Robert Waring affectionately. 'Go on. Burn the midnight oil for a change.'

'I must get to my bed. You know how gloomy I am if I

54

keep late hours,' she said, faintly smiling. 'God bless.'

She left the room quietly.

Robert Waring served Julie with some food and poured her a glass of wine. As he gave it to her he said, 'Champagne at midnight with the leading actor. French boulevard comedy, mm?'

'It's very delicious.'

'Champagne is treated with too much deference,' he said, starting his supper. 'I use half bottles to fill the conversation when I deal with *anybody* east of Vienna. It also comes in handy when I'm trying to persuade an actor to join the Royalty.'

'But no actor has to be *persuaded*,' said Julie. 'That's absurd.'

'My dear child. I know that isn't the thing to call you but that is what you are. *Every* actor worth having has to be persuaded to play anything. Actors have to be wooed with far more energy than any woman.'

Julie listened with a certain amount of wonder. It was a new idea that Sir had to persuade actors . . .

'And don't start thinking that the wooing of actors is something I alone suffer from,' he said, pointing at Julie with a chicken leg. 'Any director will tell you the same story. Of course I have a tremendous advantage at the job because *I* know how actors will behave. Who better? I behave like it myself when the film fellas are after me. Yes . . .' he went on broodingly, 'getting an actor to agree to some plum part – Iago, the Master Builder, Malvolio, you name it – is a long, predictable flirtation. You approach him. He thanks you with tears of gratitude. Then with infinite regret he refuses. How good of you to offer him the part; how he wishes he could accept. But somehow he isn't *ready*.'

'That's mad!'

'No. That's actors. The actor wants the director on his knees; he needs it for his ego, a sort of spiritual Vitamin C. Later on, you mournfully accept his refusal. Later still he writes – actors always prefer letters – to say he's thought it over. The saga continues. In the end, you get him,' said Robert Waring succinctly, and finished the leg of chicken.

Julie asked questions which made him chuckle. Why didn't Sir Robert turn the actor down and get another?

'Because there isn't another. There are a lot of actors of course. But the real talent . . . mm . . . that's rare. And the ones who've got it, know it. So they should.'

55

They had finished their meal and the champagne, and the candles were burning low; one of them caught the petals of a rose alight and Julie blew it out. The candle smoked, 'like incense at an altar,' remarked Robert Waring.

He walked over, with the stride that on-stage had often reminded Julie of a panther's, and switched on some music on the stereo. A voice began to sing a simple melody to the accompaniment of a sitar.

Sitting down beside her, he remarked, 'You didn't want to come and stay with me, did you?'

What was the use of telling a polite lie? He was too clever and he'd guessed the truth. She turned, smiling, to look at him. His beautiful face was familiar now, with its high cheek bones and long lustrous eyes. And Julie had the oddest feeling just then. It was as if a dark landscape was suddenly illumined by a flash of lightning. She thought: I don't believe you are going to disappear from my life after all.

'No. I didn't want to come,' she said slowly. 'It was very kind of you to ask me.'

'Oh dear. Those politenesses. I wish you'd forget them. They're quite a change, of course. The members of your generation are sometimes damned rude. Damned talented, too, of course,' he added, growling slightly.

He stared at his elegant shoes. 'So you didn't want to come. Frightened of me?'

'Not very. Not now.'

'What a pity.'

'Well, everybody's slightly frightened of you,' conceded Julie, laughing. She was more confident now; it was so late and so quiet, the champagne fizzed inside her, the handsome man staring at his shoes was infinitely relaxed.

'I try to keep 'em frightened,' he remarked. 'It's handy.'

'I don't believe you always mean to. You're alarming whether you want to be or not.'

He raised his eyebrows sardonically. He looked at her. She was wearing a white blouse and a floppy black bow, the kind worn by a nineteenth-century artist. It didn't suit her, he thought; she should wear colours to make her glow. But her clothes had the advantage of simplicity and he approved of that. He approved still more of her round expressive face framed in long curling hair, her pretty mouth, her hoarse little voice; ah, he liked that voice.

'Tell me why you didn't want to stay with me.'

'Don't absolutely fall about if I tell you, will you, Sir Robert?'

'Can't promise that.'

Julie thought : No, I suppose one could never ask you not to laugh if you wanted to. Mirth was always somewhere near him; laughter was his angel or his familiar, his good or his bad. He was haunted by laughter.

'You did guess right. I didn't want to come,' she said. 'Though it *is* amazingly good of you, whatever you may say! I didn't want to stay here because you are you. Chris – he's my friend, an ASM at the Sheridan – says you're out of our league. You are. You're too big for people like us. You make things sort of . . .'

'Dwindle?' he suggested helpfully.

'Yes,' she said. 'Yes. And since I don't want to creep about like Brutus said everybody did with Julius Caesar.'

'Gentle heaven, woman, it is *Cassius* who makes that speech :

"Why, man, he doth bestride the narrow world
Like a Colossus; and we petty men
Walk under his huge legs, and peep about
To find ourselves dishonourable graves." '

Her teasing companion of supper-time was gone. As he spoke the over-quoted words, Shakespeare's power was in them.

Julie said, 'Oh, please go on.'

He scratched his nose. 'You'd like a *rendition*, wouldn't you? A little private request performance. And then you'd take your candlestick, as Henry James would say, and trip up to bed and avoid discussing why you practically refused my enticing invitation.'

She laughed because, of course, he made her. They talked a little more about Julie's scruples, her caution, Sir Robert had already detected that trait of hers. He dismissed her remarks as absurd. Why shouldn't she give him twenty-four hours of her company, merely because 'he was unfortunate enough to be famous?'

That made her laugh too.

Long before Julie had begun to be tired, Robert Waring had switched off the record player. He escorted her up the staircase to a cool, pretty room overlooking the garden.

He said good night.

'Harry will come in with your breakfast. Don't get up until

57

she calls you. Now God bless.'

He gave her a grin as if they shared a small conspiracy of some kind. He shut the door.

It was only when she was alone that Julie knew how tired she was.

There was a tap at her door, and Julie awoke to see the sun edging the curtains; it was morning. When she called 'Come in', Harriet Waring appeared with a breakfast tray. Harriet set the tray down, pulled back the curtains, and the sun came flooding in like a warm golden river. Julie sat up and yawned and smiled.

Harriet thought what a child she looked, sitting up in the big bed, wearing an old-fashioned nightdress with a high neck and long sleeves.

'Good morning, Julie. I hope you slept well? Some of our visitors complain that the bed's hard.'

'It's gorgeous and I slept like a log. Is it early?'

'Earlyish,' said Harriet. Julie looked at her watch and saw it was after eleven.

'I feel very guilty at sleeping late and being given breakfast in bed.'

'Please don't be,' Harriet said, with her tired smile. 'Sir is never up until one o'clock. He does most of his telephoning . . . he lives on the telephone . . . in the morning from his bed. Tam says he directs campaigns from his bed like Napoleon.'

She came over to pour out Julie's coffee. Julie noticed her hands, which were as elegant as her brother's.

'And how is my Tam?' Harriet said, lingering for a moment. 'I haven't been down to see *Much Ado* yet. They say you and Tam are both good. I hope to come this week; is Tam well?'

'Bubbling and bouncing.'

Harriet looked amused. 'That's Tam all right. I should imagine she makes rather a rumbustious dressing-room companion. She has her father's high spirits. You haven't met Candida yet, have you? She's three years older than Tam, of course, but I always say that Candida is the gentle one . . .'

'I've seen her act, of course,' murmured Julie.

'Yes. Isn't it funny how easily she makes one cry?' said Harriet. 'It's quite annoying when she does it in real life. You'll like Candida,' she added, looking down at Julie. 'I must go. Don't hurry to get up, please. Luncheon isn't until two.'

She gave Julie a smile that had a gleam of the Warings in it somewhere.

Julie's bedroom was rather rich, with a fine eighteenth-century landscape on the wall, and Victorian silver hairbrushes on the dressing-table. She breakfasted lazily, had a slow bath in the peacock blue bathroom which was carpeted in white and tiled like a Spanish garden. She thought about Sir. She imagined him sitting up in some vast Imperial bed, telephoning instructions to a waiting populace. Then she remembered what he'd told her last night, 'actors have to be wooed.' It took an effort of Julie's imagination to rearrange Sir so that he spent Sunday morning cooing like a dove over the telephone to some actor who didn't want to work for him.

He *says* that's what he does. Somehow I don't believe it, Julie thought.

She decided to wear the dress she'd bought with her first week's salary at the Sheridan; it was patterned in pink and green, and had small buttons and pleats. Julie did her face and combed her hair a different way, plaiting it high and leaving the plait to fall down from the back of her head. Tam had suggested the style which Julie knew suited her.

It was long after midday when Julie left her bedroom and walked down the corridor. There were pictures everywhere. Sickert. Augustus John. Early French engravings. A sketch of Sir in *Julius Caesar* as Cassius. Julie remembered the four lines spoken last night. She reached the top of the staircase under a high skylight through which bright sunshine shone.

The Waring house, symbolically, seemed full of light. Down in the main hall the doors of the rooms were all open and sunshine flooded in, reflected in polished floors, white walls, mirrors and polished furniture. A vase of roses almost four feet tall stood on a marble table; carefully arranging the flowers was a dark girl in a white overall.

As Julie walked down the stairs the girl said with a smile, and speaking in a very Italian accent, 'Is in the garden.'

'Thank you,' said Julie, thinking '*Who* is? As if I need to ask.'

The garden of the Waring house was a series of lawns and terraces, sloping steeply and ending in a little orchard. Seated under a crab-apple tree near the top terrace, with a garden table in front of him covered in papers, was Sir. A large honey-coloured dog sat beside him.

'Julie,' called Sir, the moment she came on to the terrace. 'Come and have a glass of my special. Orange juice, mint and ice.'

He patted the garden seat beside him, adding : 'Let me introduce Sheba. She is also a Waring. To the end of her tail.'

The dog, a golden retriever, moved over to Julie, politely sniffed her hand and returned to her master, sitting down with a graceful flop.

'I know Sheba already,' Julie said. 'She was in your production of *Two Gentlemen of Verona*. She played Crab.'

'*All* actors' dogs play Crab sooner or later,' said Robert Waring, 'though I'll admit Sheba's performance was good. She showed a nice sense of comedy. She had quite a bit of fan mail, didn't you, girl?'

Robert Waring then looked at Julie and remarked that he did not need to ask if she had slept well.

'You look as fresh as a daisy,' he said critically. 'As fresh as the morning. Just as well,' he added significantly.

Julie, accepting a long glass of orange juice and mint leaves, decided not to ask what he meant. She had known Sir for a few days now; a few days which seemed like a few centuries. And she was at last beginning to get the hang of his conversation. Talking to Sir was a game of leap-frog in which Sir jumped *over* his opponent; for you had to get used to the fact that in any talk with Sir an opponent was what you became.

Tam and David turned up for lunch which was served with formality in the large dining-room. It was a room, thought Julie, which might have belonged to a duke in the last century. The furniture was dark and shiny, there was a lot of silver, and inevitable portraits of Sir stared down at them.

Lunch itself was enjoyable. Everybody talked spiritedly and there was a lot of laughter. Afterwards the family had coffee under the crab-apple tree, served by the pretty Italian girl Julie had met earlier.

The sunny afternoon began to grow late, and the shadows were long on the lawn. Julie thought : My week-end is almost over. Sir and Tam had wandered off to a grassy path between the flower-beds where they paced up and down, deep in conversation. David Bryden sat in a deck-chair reading the Sunday papers. Harriet, wearing an old straw hat, was busy picking the dead heads off the roses which grew in a long bed edged with lavender.

Although traffic hummed in the distance, the hum of bees was louder. The unfamiliar and exquisite English sunshine shone down and Julie thought of Daniel. She'd be seeing him in a few hours now . . . she was longing to see him. The last time had been in the wood; she still remembered the beautiful kisses they had exchanged, before that wild, mad rush to the car and to the theatre. She thought : I'll tell him about Sir and our talks together. Daniel will be amused. She peeped at her wrist-watch and saw that it was half past four. Daniel would be telephoning at six and coming to collect her.

'Do you know Sir's number, Daniel?' Julie had asked anxiously during their race to· the theatre yesterday.

'Yes, I do. I've got it although it's ex-directory. Tam gave it to me when she was staying at home with him recently. I have met Sir a couple of times so he won't take me for some eager actor on his tracks when I telephone you,' Daniel had said.

Still thinking about Daniel, Julie walked over to Harriet and asked if she could help with the roses.

'I like gardening. I do it at home with my parents.'

'That's kind of you, Julie. I love these bushes; I planted them years ago,' Harriet murmured. She broke off more faded roses and dropped them into a basket on the grass. Busy at her task and without glancing up, Harriet said : 'I think Sir wants a chat with you, Julie. I expect he'll ask you to go into his study with him later. He prefers to talk indoors; he always says nature's a "damned distraction".'

Julie was nonplussed and when Harriet turned round and smiled, all Julie could think to say was a weak 'Oh.'

'You aren't nervous of a talk with him, surely? I should think you'd enjoy it. Actresses always do.'

'Of course,' said Julie, assuming the right note of reverence. It would not have fooled Sir for one minute but Harriet looked gratified and murmured good, she would bring tea in about five o'clock. And look, Sir was beckoning.

She *lives* for him. It's disgraceful; doesn't she have a life of her own at all? thought Julie indignantly.

Sir, indeed, was beckoning imperiously to Julie. Tam and David were leaving, he said, and wanted to say goodbye.

Tam, holding a large bunch of roses that her father had

cut for her (he gives them to all the girls! thought Julie)
kissed Julie briefly.

'See you in church. Hero darling'. Bye-bye, Sheba, you
gorgeous girl.'

The dog waved her long tail with pleasure.

'We must rush,' Tam said. 'Crowds of David's friends
descending. 'Bye, Dad. 'Bye, Harry.'

'Cheerio,' said David, taking Tam's arm. They went off
through the garden.

Robert Waring stood, arms folded, listening to the sound
of David's car starting up and then roaring away down the
hill.

'Good,' he said to Julie. 'I always expect the car to turn
round and come back. Tam usually forgets something she
terms "vital" and I consider insignificant. Now, Julie, we can
concentrate on one another. Did Harry tell you I want you to
step into my parlour? Come along, child.'

Julie followed him meekly across the grass.

Robert Waring's study was on a considerably smaller scale
than the rest of the Hampstead house. It had a large desk and
two telephones but it was cosy. It was lined with books from
floor to ceiling; there was a set of library steps so that you
could climb up to the top shelf to reach the volumes. The
walls were covered in framed photographs and designs. Near
the french windows was a small sofa covered in green
taffeta.

'Sit down, Julie. Harry will bring us tea in a little while.'

Julie sat on the sofa and Robert Waring took a large high-
backed chair facing her.

'Relax, Julie. You're sitting like a visiting Royal!'

She tried to look comfortable but didn't succeed. She felt as
if she were being interviewed by a particularly authoritative
headmaster. Robert Waring's dictatorial manner daunted her.

Unaware of the unflattering image, he rubbed his nose and
said abruptly, 'Margery Wylie didn't sign you up for her next
production, the Noel Coward, did she?'

'No.'

'Disappointed?'

'Very,' said Julie, her voice hoarser than usual. She cleared
her throat.

Robert Waring picked up a paper knife shaped like a
rapier. He pointed the sharp end towards her.

'I'm not sure you're right for Noel Coward. His women
have to look like boards, wearing those thirties clothes. Hip-

less women. *You* have hips.'

'I could lose weight!' exclaimed Julie, stung.

'You may have to,' was the annoying reply.

Once again, as so often before, Julie did not ask what he meant. But oh, she *did* wonder. Tam said her father never did anything on impulse and always worked everything out in advance. Had he decided to offer Julie something after all? Might he, perhaps, suggest her as a walk-on in his new Brecht series? Or give her the chance to audition for the Royalty's experimental theatre in North London? According to Chris, the actors who worked there had to learn circus acrobatics.

If Sir would give me a chance, I'd swing from a trapeze, thought Julie desperately. After feeling so relaxed all the week-end, she was suddenly tense.

Robert Waring walked over to the window, frowned at a sparrow hopping on the terrace, turned round and came back to Julie. She still sat bolt-upright on the sofa.

'Do you like Bernard Shaw?' he said suddenly.

Julie forgot to feel tense and answered, 'I *love* him.'

'That's quite a change,' he said. 'A lot of the young don't dig Shaw. Tam and Candida are very prejudiced about him. Say he's dated. Of course he is. Only Shakespeare doesn't date. Well . . . I'll grant you Chekov. But Shaw is a dated genius. Well now, Miss Julie Woods,' he added, looking at the solemn little figure on the sofa, 'you will have gathered I have a proposition to put to you.'

She swallowed and said nothing.

'I'd like you to try *Joan* in my new production.'

There was a silence like a clap of thunder.

Robert Waring looked at her quizzically.

'Me?' croaked Julie at last. 'Saint Joan?'

'I took you by surprise again, I see. I do nothing but astound you, Julie. You spend your time gazing at me like a child watching a conjurer. Yes, I think with a deal of hard work and some tears I can get a very passable *Joan* out of you. There's something about you. Just right.'

He looked at her detachedly as if he were a sculptor; with a piece of clay, perhaps.

'Something stubborn. Cautious. Dedicated. Solemn. Funny, now and again. Brave, I would say. I knew it when I saw your Hero. Well? What do you say?'

There was a gentle knock at the door before Julie could reply; Harriet came in carrying the tea tray. She glanced

63

from her brother to the pale girl facing him. She'd seen that scene played before. She picked up the silver tea pot and poured out their tea. Deliberately, she cut Julie a thick slice of home-made cake.

'Quite right, Harry. She needs that. Hot sweet tea and cake. She's just had a bad shock,' said Robert Waring and burst out laughing.

The rest of the afternoon Julie and Robert Waring spent talking about *Saint Joan*. He told her his idea of the production, how soon it was to be announced, made plans for Julie to come to London the moment *Much Ado* was finished. In the meantime she was to start work immediately and read, not only Shaw's play, but everything about Joan of Arc she could lay her hands on.

'Try the local library for the time being. Later you can do some work on her at the British Museum,' he said. 'You'll discard nine-tenths of what you read, of course, but you've got to know *everything*. Let's see . . .' he added, looking at the carriage clock on the shelf, 'it's just on six. We'll work until ten, then Harry will join us for a late supper. I'll drive you down to the Sheridan tomorrow at lunch-time. Right?'

He gave her a smile which was quite different from his usual sardonic grin; it was the look of a man who was sharing his work with her.

Julie had been conscious of the carriage clock for over an hour and she said desperately, 'I'm so very sorry, Sir Robert, but I can't stay this evening. I've promised to meet someone.'

Robert Waring didn't have time to reply though his face expressed exaggerated amazement. For just at that moment the telephone rang.

Julie *knew* it was Daniel.

Robert Waring picked up the telephone and answered smoothly.

'Yes? Daniel Monteith? Ah yes, of course I remember you. We met at Tamara's flat, I think. Julie Woods? Yes, she's in the garden. I'll get her . . .'

He pointed at Julie, indicating she should go out on to the terrace.

He put down the telephone and followed her.

Julie, relieved to be out of earshot of Daniel, Daniel whom she'd been longing to see all day, began eagerly, 'Sir Robert, I did promise faithfully I'd meet him. Could I rush out for half an hour and explain? I won't be long. I only want to – '

'Out of the question,' he interrupted. 'Not to be considered. I'm so sorry,' he added cheerfully. 'I understand it is hard to start rearranging your plans. And only an hour after being offered the best chance of your life. However, there it is. There's no choice, is there? Run along in and tell your friend you'll be in touch.'

'But suppose I was only ten – '

'Julie. Do not waste our time in argument,' he said coolly. And she felt a mouse indeed, facing the lion of lions.

'Run along,' he repeated, and strolled over to pick a piece of rosemary from a tall bush growing by the window.

Julie trailed indoors.

'Daniel?'

'Julie! Dearest girl! Will quarter to seven be all right? I'm so sorry to be late but I've had to wait around for some reference books all day – Clover's just arrived with them. I can be with you in just over half an hour . . .'

His voice was deep and loving. It hurt her.

'I can't come tonight, Daniel. I'm so disappointed – I wish I could come! But a job has turned up, an extraordinary one, I'll tell you all about it when we meet. Could we see each other this week? Any evening or lunch-time or any time? I'm so sorry about tonight. I know you'll understand.'

Silence.

Then he said, 'Do you?'

'Daniel. You're not angry, are you?'

'Not in the least. I quite understand that a job has turned up, as you put it. Which is exactly what I told you that Sir Robert was up to in the first place. I must go. It won't be necessary to wish you good luck. Clearly, *yours* has arrived.'

He rang off.

3

It was the last night of *Much Ado*. The play had only run a month but at the final performance the actors had the same heightened mood they would have shared had it run twice as long. It was the play, its wit and sparkle, which bound them together and it was this union that was about to snap.

The last performance had been sold out for days, the theatre was packed to the roof. At the end the applause was a huge wave, drenching the actors with noise and kindness. They bowed and laughed, bowed and smiled, ran off the stage, and came back to bow again.

Backstage after the performance the mood continued; everybody was in a kissing, tearful, joky, abandoned frame of mind. Dressing-room doors stood open and actors hung around, drinking wine and forgetting to pack.

Julie rustled down the corridor wearing her Hero dress for the last time. John Locking, who had played Benedick, was standing at his door.

'Our little Hero,' he said sentimentally, putting his arm out to encircle her as she went by. 'Come and have a farewell drink. I want the chance to thank you for your marvellous support. For everything. Everything,' he repeated and looked at her with real – if momentary – affection.

She stayed and smiled but she didn't feel at home in the noisy dressing-room. Actors raced in and out like cheerful travellers full of jokes and plans. In the talk and laughter about the immediate future, nobody asked Julie where *she* was going next week. Perhaps they thought she would be out of work and didn't want to hurt her feelings . . .

It was ironic that she couldn't tell them what had happened to her. Robert Waring had impressed on her that she must keep the enormous secret to herself. He would announce it soon as part of his release about the season. In the meantime – silence.

Julie, looking round the crowded dressing-room, had an idea that some of the actors wouldn't be exactly pleased if they knew who had given her a job . . . and such a job. So she said goodbye and climbed the stairs to the dressing-room she'd shared with Tam.

She had bought a little end-of-the-production present for Tam: a china pomander that smelled of cloves. Julie knew Tam collected pomanders. She was looking forward to giving it to Tam, whose reactions to Julie were always immediate – and warm. But when she came into the dressing-room she was surprised to find it deserted.

Across Tam's mirror was scrawled in thick white eye-pencil: 'Sorry, darlin' had to go with David. TV wants him or something!! Terrible rush. See you in London.

'Luv. Luv. T.'

66

Julie stood crestfallen in the deserted room, feeling like a girl on the last day of term. The room smelled of Tam's resinous scent, of make-up, of a certain musty silky smell from their heavy costumes lined with buckram. Tam's Beatrice dress, yellow silk and pearls, lay across the table; the way it was thrown, half hanging to the ground, showed just how much its wearer had been in a hurry. Beside it were tossed the long red plaits, Tam's great necklace of yellow stones, her rings, her fan. The dressing-room was abandoned. The player was gone.

Julie took off her costume, showered and changed, arranged her wig on the wig-stand and placed her jewellery beside it.

I should feel excited. I only feel sad and scared, she thought. She collected the belongings that had accumulated during her stay here: first-night telegrams and paperbacks, the shabby Koala bear she'd had since a child and which she said brought her luck. Under a pile of magazines she found a script. It was *Half in Half*, David Bryden's new play which Tam was rehearsing at present. Written on it in bold handwriting was 'Daniel Monteith'.

Daniel had given her the script last week, saying, 'Read it soon and tell me what you think when we meet. Don't forget, Julie. I'll be fascinated. I'll ask you the moment we meet so you'd better hurry up and read it tonight after the performance!'

Then, Daniel had spoken of them both in the future. 'When we meet,' he'd said. *Now*, a week away, she had not seen or spoken to him. He'd gone as completely as if she'd never known him; simply disappeared out of her life. And Tam, who was working with him and her husband on the new play, had pointedly not mentioned him to Julie.

She put the script in her suitcase and was emptying some dead roses out of a vase when Chris came in.

'Julie!' he said, pleased. 'I sho' am glad to see you, gal! I was getting offended; thought you'd roared off with Tam without saying goodbye. Can I drive you back to London?'

'*Drive* me, Chris?'

'Yeah. The bird in the box office has lent me her Mini for the week-end. She had to go home to her Mum and Dad and I was rather pathetic about my luggage. Let's drive back to our digs and pick up all our stuff, shall we? We don't want to hang around here; gives me the willies when it's over. I shall need a lot of cheerful chat to keep me going on the journey.

Let's take some hot cocoa in a thermos. My grandfather used to say cocoa makes one sweat but it never does me. Still, he was a dancer and they sweat like pigs . . .'

Julie's melancholy mood was lightened by Chris's mischievous face. Exclaiming over his depression at leaving the Sheridan, he looked cheerful, even hilarious.

'Do stop emptying those flower vases, girl! This is not a graveyard though that's how I'm viewing it at present. A graveyard of hopes. Ha ha!' said Chris. 'Someone left a bottle of cider in one of the dressing-rooms. Shall we take that too?'

It was after three in the morning when they finally arrived in London. They had packed at their digs, which had taken longer than they imagined, had difficulty in locating a garage open after midnight for petrol, and driven the two-hour journey without any supper. The heater in the Mini wasn't working and they both felt freezing cold. Chris's high spirits were flagging. A girl he knew had lent him some digs, he explained; she was away on tour and the rent was paid. All Chris's friends were like that; they showered him with free accommodation and cars and help with jobs; even Julie had sewn buttons on his shirts.

Chris wasn't too sure of the location of the digs, which were 'somewhere Swiss-Cottagey'. He drove around for twenty minutes before he finally found the road and the house.

'You can stay here as long as I do, Julie. My friend has two rooms and as the place is crawling with people it'll be quite respectable. I mean there's at least a dozen of us!' said Chris, peering at a tall Victorian house to be sure he had the number right.

They went up the steps carrying their luggage. The door, painted black, was sombre; the pillared portico had seen better days. Chris suddenly discovered he had lost the front door key; he thought this a great joke and stood stifling giggles while he went through every pocket.

Julie didn't give him any words of encouragement or even laugh; she was too tired and cold. She just stood, thinking in a vague, exhausted way that Sir Robert must be asleep somewhere in that beautiful house. What did Sir dream about? thought Julie, yawning.

'Got it!' cried Chris triumphantly. 'In we go. Don't fall over the cat.'

'Is there a cat?' whispered Julie, as they crept into the dark house.

68

'How should I know?' he hissed back.

They went up a dark staircase, passing many closed doors. Chris took her across a landing and located his friend's two rooms . . . he had been here once before. He opened one of the doors and they stepped into an enormous, cheerless room with a ceiling as high as an assembly hall.

Chris switched on a light in a dim green shade.

'Golly, it's freezing,' he said. 'We'll get pneumonia. No we won't, we can drink our cocoa. And I *think* Sal told me where she hides her electric fire. Was it on top of the wardrobe?'

He dragged a chair across the room, put up his hand and said 'It was.'

They crouched by a one-bar fire, sipping the cocoa which had been brewed by kindly far away Mrs White.

There was a little silence.

'I'm sorry I'm a bit low, Chris,' Julie said, glancing at the cheerful figure hunched beside her. 'You're sweet to me; I never thank you.'

'It's a draggy place, isn't it?' he said with relish. 'Quite the House of Spooks, Cert X. But you don't care, Sir won't let you stay here long. Not nearly smart enough for his new Saint Joan.'

'*Who told you*!'

Gratified at her horror and astonishment, he blew on his cocoa.

'I've known for days. And I don't reveal my sources, as reporters say. I'd be a fool if I did. Anyway, I think it's super about you and he's a clever old Sir after all. I trust you won't go all strange when you're famous, by the way. I've known some that did.'

'I'm not famous and the idea's ridiculous anyway.'

'Isn't it? But I shan't let you,' he said comfortably. 'And now you'd better go to bed or you'll look *repulsive* tomorrow.'

The following day was dampish. Julie spent it hanging about with nothing to do. Chris was still asleep after she was up and dressed and she didn't like to knock on his door and disturb him. For all his bright spirits, he'd looked exhausted last night and Julie left him in peace, but without him she was lonely and at a loose end.

It wasn't the big gloomy house that was lonely; on the contrary it was full of cheerful people who looked as if they might be actors or models. They answered telephones, ran up and down stairs, slammed doors, burst out laughing, and played loud radios. But Julie didn't know them and was too shy to get into conversation. Once or twice she went down to the telephone in the hall and tried to get through to her agent to find whether she was meant to go to the Royalty to attend a first rehearsal. But her agent's number was permanently engaged or out of order.

The day dragged by. She went out in the drizzle of early evening and had eggs and chips in a local café. She returned at an even looser end, wondering how to spend the long evening.

Chris was probably going to sleep right on through until the next morning. He had the habit of making up on sleep when he had the chance; of replacing all those nights as assistant stage manager when he was working up until dawn. 'When I get some real sleep, I wallow!' Chris once said.

Julie felt she couldn't wake him, and trailed up the stairs to her room, and sat on the bed staring into space. It was all very well pretending she actually liked the high-ceilinged room Chris had been kind enough to find for her. But she didn't. And it was all very fine coming to London to take up a marvellous new job. But where was it? Nobody from the Royalty had contacted her and there was no word from her agent. Julie felt she was in a kind of limbo.

She wandered down the stairs again to try her agent just once more. Surely *he'd* know where she was to go and whether her contract had been signed. He'd been enthusiastic enough when she told him about it. What had happened to him? Why hadn't he been in touch with her?

Suddenly, when she picked up the telephone, on impulse she dialled Tam's number instead. She stood listening to the number ring and ring again; she was just about to put the receiver down when a voice bright as new money said, 'Yes?'

'Tam. It's Julie. I only rang to say hallo.'

'*Julie*! My God, woman, where ARE you? My father has been bellowing at me down the telephone like a demented bull! He has rung *five times*. He is ab-so-lu-tely *furious*!'

'What do you mean? Furious with whom?' asked Julie, alarmed.

'With me for losing you! With you for disappearing! He said I should have brought you to London with me last night and kept an eye on you. Or fixed for him to send a car for you. You name it, Julie, and I didn't do it! And as for what he said about *you*. You're the first actress he ever signed up IN HIS LIFE who promptly vanished into thin air. Where

70

are you, for the love of heaven?'

'Swiss Cottage.'

'WHAT ARE YOU DOING THERE?' cried Tam. 'Come round right away. Let me explain how you get here . . . and listen carefully, Julie, because I'm not answerable for your life or mine if you don't turn up safely within the next twenty minutes!'

Julie scribbled a note to Chris which she pushed under his door. Throwing frugal principles to the wind, she took the first taxi which came down the road and gave Tam's address in Hampstead.

The taxi drew up, after a short journey, at the entrance to what had been a series of stables built around a cobbled court-yard. Two of the stables had been converted into an attractive, odd-shaped house, with a wooden staircase running up the outside and large picture windows shining with lights in the dusk.

Julie paid the taxi, and walked up the staircase. A door at the top of the steps opened. And there was Tam.

'Julie! Come in, come in. I rang Dad with the good news but he's gone out to dinner. I expect you'll have ruined his digestion. Anyway I told Harriet who said we can both relax.'

Tam led the way into a room which at first sight seemed entirely the colour of golden syrup. The effect was made by wood; shiny wooden floors, walls of planks the same rich colour; the place glowed. A low sofa was heaped with cushions, and there were books, paintings, rugs, cushions and photographs everywhere. A large study of Sir as Hamlet fixed them with accusing eyes.

'Sit down, darlin'. I couldn't believe it when I heard your voice just now. The relief,' said Tam, pouring drinks. 'Push that cushion out of the way,' she added hospitably. 'And try this drink, it's David's special and has orange juice in it.'

Tam stood sparkling at Julie like champagne. Julie felt quite dazzled; by Tam, by the room and the lights, and most of all by the welcome after her long day of rain and solitude.

'Before Dad rings, let's get our story straight. Where have you been since the curtain came down on *Much Ado* last night?' Tam asked.

'With Chris. At some digs.'

'But why didn't you . . .?'

Julie explained about her agent. Tam listened and giggled.

'It makes perfect sense now, but it didn't when Dad rang. He was outraged. You didn't leave your address at the Sheridan, you know (rather unprofessional of you), and Sir kept thundering "Don't argue. Find her!" I didn't know where to start. Norman at the stage door said you'd gone off to a party with John Locking . . . that didn't sound right somehow. I kept ringing your agent and of course I couldn't get through either. I tried Mrs White at your digs but she was out for the day. Ah well; all over now. Still, you'd better be prepared for fireworks when you see Dad!' she added, and laughed heartlessly.

She cooked an omelette and made coffee and they sat on the huge settee and talked shop and more shop. Julie was glad to be with Tam, and enjoyed the evening. But she did notice how delicately Tam skated over the subject of Daniel. Who had asked Tam so particularly not to talk about Daniel to her? Perhaps he himself.

During supper she told Tam about the digs and about her drive to London last night with Chris, adding that she felt rather guilty enjoying herself, while poor Chris was so tired he was sleeping through an entire day.

'Pooh. Don't feel sorry for Chris,' said Tam. 'He's the guy who's all right whatever happens. Haven't you noticed? If there is a flood, some bird throws Chris a plank, and if there's a fire, an entire bevy of birds holds a blanket for him to jump into. Forget about Chris. The man for *you* to worry about is my Dad!'

'You mean because he is angry with me?'

'I mean because he's involved with you. Anybody Dad takes on needs nerves of steel.'

'How are yours?' asked Julie.

'Terrible,' said Tam, jumping guiltily as the telephone rang. All the evening, when Tam's busy telephone shrilled, both girls started up in alarm. Every time they thought there was a step on the outside staircase, they exchanged anxious looks. But no Sir appeared like offended Jove. No Sir thundered on the telephone. They drank coffee and played the record player and Harriet rang very late to say would Tam tell Julie there was a meeting, and Director's Notes, at Hampstead at ten sharp. Would Julie be prompt, please. Julie was convinced she was now in the Waring bad books.

'Don't go taxi-ing back to Swiss Cottage. Stay the night with me,' Tam suggested. 'David's in Amsterdam seeing about the Dutch version of *Half* (it's coming on next month); I'd love to have your company. We've heaps of room,' she added, indicating the sofa.

But Julie thanked her and said it was very kind but she ought to get back. 'Chris did get me the digs and he might be hurt.'

'Sentimentalist!' said Tam. 'A few weeks of Sir and he'll change all that!'

Julie was almost ready for her Hampstead appointment next morning when Chris finally appeared. He came into her room, yawning and rubbing his eyes, wearing an old towelling bathrobe, with his curly hair in spikes.

'Hi, Julie, what a *marvellous* sleep I had. I could sleep till the crack of doom. Did you have a dire day without me?'

'It wasn't too bad. It rained mostly.'

'Poor you. You should have slept like me. Did your agent ring? How's the contract?'

'I'm off to rehearsal,' said Julie unnecessarily.

Chris, who knew actresses, smiled slightly. It was so obvious where she was going; he could see it in her make-up, the way her hair was done, her trouser suit, her nervous, over-brilliant manner.

He yawned again and looked round the cheerless room. Julie had made her bed and covered it with the thin brown silk cover. There was nothing on the mantelpiece but her handbag. It was a vast marble mantelpiece, meant to hold Victorian photographs in silver frames, vases of dried grasses, clocks, ivory elephants, pipe cleaners, pin cushions. It was empty. So was the chest of drawers, and the wardrobe, both of which should have held petticoats and ball gowns.

'It's not bad, this room,' he said critically. 'It's jolly good for the money except that she's paid it and we're getting it free. Oh, by the way,' added Chris, 'before you go, Julie, I may be seeing Daniel Monteith today. I said I might go round to his studio for a chat about a job. He was rather kind. Any messages?'

Julie turned away to take her handbag from the mantelpiece and said quite cheerfully, 'No messages.'

She said goodbye to Chris who trailed after her into the corridor, wishing her luck. He immediately saw a pretty girl who was passing, carrying a paper bag full of shopping, and began to chat to her.

Julie hurried downstairs and out into the morning street.

She took a bus, which stopped at the bottom of a hill some distance away from the Waring house. The conductor shouted

'All change' and Julie had to walk the rest of the way. But she had given herself ample time. She walked up the road with its avenue of young chestnuts, and arrived at the gate of the Waring house a good quarter of an hour early.

As she went through the gate, she noticed that the garden was full of flowers. The flower-beds were crowded with plants and shrubs damp from the rain, blossoming and budding in thick profusion; there were early lupins and a border of white pinks, bushes of strong pink roses and late forget-me-nots. The last time she'd seen forget-me-nots they had been wild ones growing in the wood where Daniel had kissed her. She despised herself for that thought. She needed to be resolute and bright now, and the small blue flowers made her suddenly achingly sad.

The Italian girl called Mia opened the front door and greeted Julie hospitably.

'Good morning. Is in the study waiting.'

Help! thought poor Julie.

She followed the girl, quaking, down the corridor to Robert Waring's study door.

Sir Robert was standing with his back to the room, looking out of the open french window, his hands clasped behind him. He was dressed in dark brown velvet, rather an old suit, rather a becoming one. He turned and frowned.

'Here you are,' he said with exaggerated surprise. 'Come in, please. Rehearsal is in fifteen minutes.'

'I'm sorry. Am I early?'

'You are twenty-four hours late. Sit down. No, not on that settee; last time you were here I was convinced you were going to slip off it. Take the chair,' he said, pointing to a large leather chair facing him. Julie sat down. He remained standing, surveying her.

Julie had not seen Sir in anything but a sparkling, kindly mood; this morning his mouth was thin, his manner definitely sarcastic.

'Tamara informs me that you spent the day at some lodgings or other,' he said. 'Why?'

In spite of her determination to remain well behaved and even apologetic for the misunderstanding, Julie found herself getting annoyed. He stood confronting her; he might, she thought, have been a detective.

'Sir Robert,' she said, mild but firm, 'I'm not really twenty-four hours late.'

'Of course you are.'

'But how can I be? You and I had no appointment.'

As she had expected, he threw his great eyes upwards as if dealing with somebody very stupid.

'But we didn't,' Julie said, still mildly, though she was really irritated by now. 'You gave me – yes, you gave me a marvellous opportunity. I was, and am, knocked sideways by it. But we didn't make a single arrangement. I told my agent what you'd said to me –'

'The man's a fool!'

'Told him what you'd said,' continued Julie firmly. 'But yesterday when I tried to get through to him his number was engaged all the time, or maybe it was out of order. What could I do? One cannot exactly telephone *you*.'

'Why not?' he enquired, twisting an eyebrow at her. He was apparently rather pleased that she felt it impossible to telephone him. His words, however, continued to be sarcastic.

'One would have thought you were *slightly* interested in when we were going to meet. One would have hoped you would even be *slightly* anxious.'

Clearly, the expected answer was a loyal, impassioned speech. She wasn't going to give one; she stared gloomily at the floor.

'We'll overlook your incompetence this once,' he said more kindly. Now he had reduced her to silence he was in a better frame of mind. 'But remember in future to keep my appointments on the nail. And how are you feeling this morning?' he went on, knowing perfectly well. 'You don't look too bright. Never mind, Julie, leave everything to me. I will look after you,' he added. His beautiful voice had completely altered in a matter of moments; one would have thought he now regarded her as the most precious thing in the world. This turn of mood was quite as unreasonable as the previous attack, and when he came over and took her hand Julie found it difficult not to scowl.

'Come along and meet the company,' he said. 'Most of them arrived hours ago. Some of them breakfasted with me. Don't look so doleful, Julie! This is a great day for you. And perhaps for me too . . .'

As she walked with him into the large drawing-room, she saw with a sharp stab of nerves that the room was crammed with people. There were at least thirty actors seated there, drinking morning coffee. There was only one other woman, a middle-aged actress sitting in a corner; every other person in the room was male. The men sat around, reminding Julie of a regiment.

And she was certain that every member of the regiment was busy summing her up.

'Good morning, Blanche – gentlemen – ' said Robert Waring, looking over at the actress and then turning to the assembled company. 'Before we start work, I must introduce you to Julie Woods. My Joan. Your Joan. Everybody's Joan,' he added, quoting *Much Ado*.

The sound of laughter surrounded Julie but she wasn't part of it. She sat holding her coffee cup, feeling two feet high and shrinking fast.

An actor sitting beside her turned and gave her a friendly smile; Julie felt slightly better.

'Julie has been playing for Margery Wylie down at the Sheridan. Some of you, I know, went down to see the production *after* you'd picked up the news; I take it you went down to take a look at Julie. News travels uncomfortably fast at the Royalty. I keep getting told about my own plans; some of them *astound* me!' said Robert Waring. 'Well, now. Here is Julie to meet us. And now, let us talk about *Saint Joan*.'

In her three years as an actress, Julie had attended many first readings, when the director of the play addressed his company, and talked about his own ideas for the production. Sometimes these Director's Notes were rather dull; you hoped for a lead, an inspiration even, all you were given was a prosy lecture. Even Margery Wylie's notes hadn't been very exciting; her ideas were sound, but brisk and practical, she had not gone deeply into the play.

Robert Waring talked for three hours which went by like a dream. The room was hushed and he stood by the fireplace, talking easily, improvising, thinking aloud. He spoke of a fifteenth-century world and of man in the dilemma of power. He talked of faith and of the strength and force of a young girl not out of her teens, who was a warrior, an angel and a martyr. People followed her but they feared her, and it was their fear that destroyed her. Joan was queen and pawn, too. He talked of life in the fifteenth century, of castles, wars, violence, nature and politics. He spoke like a man, living in those times, who'd returned for a morning to describe his life there *now*. He pointed at Julie, calling her 'This unlettered girl. This miracle. This upstart.' 'What is a martyr? Shaw

76

makes Cauchon say that mortal eyes cannot distinguish the saint from the heretic. Today, if we see a saint on television, dedicating her pure life to suffering, can we distinguish her from a frustrated bore? A prig? And doesn't she make us resent her? Shaw says that even if she came back, Joan's followers would leave her in a ditch. I think we would, too. When the play ends, the hour strikes, and Joan prays:

    'O God, that madest this beautiful earth
    When will it be ready to receive Thy Saints?
    How long, O Lord, how long?'

He stopped speaking.

There was a long silence.

Robert Waring said briskly, 'That will be all for this morning. Ladies and gentlemen, thank you for your attention. You'll find the times of rehearsals on the board at the Royalty. Tomorrow we are in the rehearsal room at ten sharp. Thank you. Thank you, everybody.' He gave the company a look which was embracing and full of warmth.

The actors rose in a body, pushed back their chairs, stubbed out cigarettes and collected the paperback copies of the play which everybody but Julie had already acquired. They began to troop out of the room, talking in low voices to each other. Julie was just going to follow them when Robert Waring came over to her.

'Come along, Julie. I want a word with you.' He led her back to his study.

She was nervous after the long morning of concentration; the task of playing Saint Joan seemed so enormous that it was impossible.

Robert Waring sat down, stretched out his legs and yawned.

'I'm tired,' he said. 'A *tour de force*. Three hours' stint. Gentle heavens. What an audience.'

'You mean wonderful?'

He stopped in the middle of a yawn and grinned.

'I mean formidable. They have to be welded into one piece, held together, unified; and it's always the beginning that counts. Very exhausting. I must stop doing it some time,' he added, scratching his head.

His face creased into a smile as he looked over at the solemn girl facing him.

'There are a number of things we must discuss, my little friend.'

'You mean about *Joan*?'

'No, Julie, I'm not talking about work just yet. We will

77

talk about the Maid later, for hours, for days. We'll begin this evening and go on until we drop. But there are other things to settle first. For instance, where you are going to live. Good, here comes Harry,' he said, as Harriet came into the room. She was followed, inevitably, by the two Italian girls carrying trays of food and drink.

The girls left the room and Harriet sat down next to her brother, who took her hand in his.

'There are one or two matters Harry and I need to discuss with you, Julie,' Robert Waring said, picking up a silver mug of celery stalks and offering it to her with the air of a man passing her a plate of something both nourishing and delicious. 'Let's start with your weight. I would judge,' he said critically, 'that you will have to lose at least half a stone, probably more. Harry, will you and Julie talk about diet and work out a schedule together? Tam's diet usually works; why not try that? Julie has only three weeks to lose it in, remember.'

He leaned over and took Julie's cheek between his thumb and forefinger.

'I want more *bones*,' he said. 'Shaw describes Joan as an able-bodied country girl but with an uncommon face, very wide-apart eyes that you see in people with a lot of imagination. I like that! Your eyes are nicely spaced, very wide apart. But I still need a face with *bones*. Joan may be able to work in the fields (although she's a young lady, not a hired help). But she's a remarkable-looking girl. And she knows how to pray. All night, if need be. So that means cheese and celery and black coffee,' he said, pouring Harriet and himself some wine.

During the brief, comfortable meal Julie forgot her nerves and began to feel relaxed; it was what the Warings wanted her to feel. Brother and sister spoke a wordless language; they understood each other intuitively. Harriet knew her brother had an enormous task to get this inexperienced raw actress to the right pitch so that she could play the central character in a masterpiece. Robert Waring was aware that he must use a particular mixture with Julie; he would need probing intelligence and persuasion, patience and impatience, a stock of guile, cajolery, a threat or two, to get what he sensed was there in Julie's latent talent.

Julie herself only felt these two had taken charge of her. During the Spartan meal she was content to be discussed as if Julie Woods were a girl at the other end of London.

'We're starting to work at once so she might as well move in here, Harry, if that suits you,' Robert Waring said.

'By far the best arrangement. Is that all right for you, Julie?' asked Harriet, her head slightly on one side as if to say kindly 'don't think we are bustling you.' Which, of course, they were.

'I do have some digs already which are quite all right,' Julie replied hesitantly.

Robert Waring raised his eyebrows.

'I'm willing to bet a pound to a penny that your digs are far from "all right",' he said. 'That isn't quite the point. You mustn't imagine we're a couple of Father Christmases, Julie, planning to make you happy. I need you here to work, work, work. And we can't waste valuable time while you move to and fro like a shuttle in a mighty loom.' The phrase amused him and he repeated 'shuttle in a mighty loom. Do you remember that motion picture I made when I was a Lancashire cotton hand, Harry?'

'Very well. You were twenty-four and looked amazing.'

'I still do,' he replied indifferently. 'So Julie is to be our house guest. That's settled.'

'There's Renfred. He's due this week,' Harriet said.

'*He* won't bother us. He's either in the city or hidden behind the *Financial Times*. You'll like Renfred, Julie; he's rich and half Hungarian and understands women. Good; Julie can move in here until we all leave for Condaford.'

'Oh – but – ' began Julie, opening her eyes wide.

The Warings turned to look at her. They waited.

'But Sir Robert, I didn't know we were doing *Joan* at Condaford! I thought it was to be at the Royalty here in London.'

'You never told her,' sighed Harriet.

'Of course I told her!' exclaimed Robert Waring. 'Of course I told her. Gentle heaven, girl, you must learn to listen.'

Sensing an atmosphere of disapproval, he said plaintively, 'How could I have avoided telling her, Harry? She knows the Repertory at the Royalty is set for six months; every actor in the country knows it. She couldn't have supposed we were going to pop a new production into a Repertory season that took a year to plan and pull off, could she?'

Harriet merely poured more coffee.

Julie had just realized the enormity of her *faux pas*. As a new player belonging to Sir's company she should have *known* she was going to Condaford. Much had been written about Sir's Condaford season in the press already; it was a new venture at a new theatre and was to be part of the drama and arts festival. Julie hadn't done her homework and she knew it. But everything had happened too quickly. It was too sudden. She hadn't coped. First meeting Daniel. Then Sir. Then the job. Then losing Daniel. It was too much . . .

'You will recall that we are opening the Condaford season in a few weeks,' Sir Robert was saying in the martyred tone of a man who had told her many times before. 'We open with *Saint Joan*. Then we're bringing in two Royalty revivals, *Henry Five* with my daughter Candida as Katharine, and *Faustus* in which I play the name part. You remember now?'

'Yes, of course. I'm so sorry. Of course.'

He accepted her apology with a nod, looked at his watch and said he must go. Was the car waiting? Had his assistant telephoned? Harriet said yes and stood up, collecting his papers and packing them deftly into his black briefcase. Sir Robert watched her with satisfaction; he liked Harriet to wait on him.

Just as he was leaving, he came over to Julie and said briefly, 'We'll begin at seven. Be ready to roll up your sleeves!' He patted her cheek, murmured, 'Half a stone at least,' and left the room with a springing step.

Julie heard the front door slam.

Harriet, who had seen him out, came back into the room looking amused. 'Now there'll be a bit of peace,' she said. 'Shall we go down to the kitchen and heat up our coffee? It's nearly cold.'

Julie followed with alacrity as they went through the house and down a narrow staircase. The basement, in fact, opened on to the lower terraces of the garden. The kitchen was spacious, with a small adjoining kitchen and scullery where the Italian girls were working and talking.

Harriet put the coffee on the stove and sat down by a big old-fashioned table on which was a bowl of marigolds.

'You mustn't mind him tugging you along at his own pace even if you think you'll never keep up,' she said. 'The only way with Sir is just to keep running as fast as you can. He's the pace-maker. He doesn't upset you, does he?'

'Not at all.'

'I'm glad. It was obvious, by the way, that he never *did* tell you about Condaford. It's something he does to me all the time. He swears he's told me some vital fact I've never heard about. The thing is that he tells *somebody,* Bernard who works with him, or one of the directors, or Tam or Candida, and there's a spirited discussion and then he tells someone *else* and by the time he gets home he automatically assumes I've heard all the talk. I'm sure without consciously knowing it he's also trying to avoid going through whatever-it-is again because talking about it has begun to bore him. He bores easily.'

'I should have read about Condaford in the papers,' Julie said uncomfortably. 'Or my agent should have told me. I do feel a fool, Harriet. But I – I was a bit overcome by everything happening so fast. And I seemed involved at the Sheridan all last week,' she added feebly. What she was really saying was 'I was miserable over Daniel all last week and hoping he would come back and knowing he would not.'

Something in her voice reached Harriet, who said, 'You must be very excited. About *Joan.*'

'More than I can say. If only I can *do* it.'

'You will.'

The door of the kitchen that led into the garden swung open and Sheba padded in. She came over and pressed her honey-coloured flanks against Harriet's knees. Harriet bent and stroked her.

'Of course one has to give up things when one is in the theatre,' she said thoughtfully. 'To make it happen, I mean. Sir does and so does Tam. Candida has always tried not to. You, I think, will have to give up things, Julie, though I don't know what those things will be. Whatever they are, if you're going to make that door open, the one that actors hammer at with their clenched fists, you will have to give things up.' And she passed Julie the coffee, which was steaming hot and black and very bitter.

Julie needed to go back to Swiss Cottage to collect her luggage, and thinking of Chris she explained to Harriet that she might be away some time. Harriet said, 'But of course, take as long as you like.' Julie found something especially relaxing about being with Harriet. She asked no questions, just gave Julie an impression, a feeling. Harriet seemed to be saying that if Julie needed anything, kindness or help, advice or hot coffee, Harriet was there for just that. But she would never, never come towards her unless it was Julie who put out her hand first.

The tall house didn't look as depressing as it had done yesterday when Julie rang the bell. The door was opened by a thin-faced girl who reminded Julie of a pretty horse; she was wearing black knickerbockers.

'Looking for Chris?' said the girl in a friendly voice. 'He's on the telephone. When is he not?'

In the dark hallway where Julie had telephoned Tam, Chris was talking animatedly. When he saw Julie he waved, put his hand over the receiver and hissed: 'Great news! Won't be long!'

Julie sat down on a window-sill nearby to wait for him. Chris went on talking and laughing. The girl in the knickerbockers ran up and down stairs, busily carrying a series of trays and glasses and mugs and plates. Apparently a party was being prepared on the first floor. The front door was ajar and a very large Australian suddenly put his head round the door and shouted : 'Got room for a little one from Melbourne?'

The knickerbocker girl gave a shriek of joy and the Australian began dragging in cardboard boxes full of beer cans.

The couple amused Julie, and when Chris finally rang off she was grinning.

Chris looked her up and down. 'Fame suits you,' he remarked. 'How's the Demon King? Don't tell me. Let me tell *you* something instead. Come on upstairs and we'll have a drink.'

'I'm not allowed to drink now, Chris.'

'Dieting! I knew he'd make you. He's famous for turning people into *skellingtons*. I bet I shan't recognize you in a week or two. So come on up and watch me have a drink. Are you staying? Shall we have supper together?'

Julie said it was very kind of Chris but she was moving into Sir's house so she could work more easily and save time. Chris looked very diverted at this, and to avoid the inevitable teasing, Julie said, 'Did you realize *Joan* is being done at Condaford? I thought it was at the Royalty. He never told me.'

'Of course it's Condaford, you ass. The Royalty season is set for . . . never mind . . . I can see somebody's already been lecturing you about your ignorance.'

They went up the dark staircase and into Chris's bedroom. He bustled over to the seven-foot wardrobe and took out a bottle of sherry, pouring a generous helping into a toothmug.

'Before you vanish off to higher planes, I've got a snippet

of news that'll please you,' he said. 'Guess what? I'm coming to Condaford too.'

'Chris, how *lovely*!'

'Isn't it?' he said complacently. 'And what is more I didn't ask you or Tam to help. A man I know who's their chief stage management person hired me. He's a bit of an old Tartar but he's always approved of me. Says I'm bright. When I heard about *Joan* and that you were going to play her, I rang him and he promised to let me know, and sure enough he telephoned last night. I'm to be his second ASM. So you won't be getting rid of your old mate after all.'

'Chris, I am *so* glad!'

She gazed at him with joyful affection and he leaned forward and grasped her hands. Both looking sixteen, they burst out laughing.

'I'm told the Condaford birds are worth looking over,' Chris added. 'There's a section of the University down there, the speech and drama bit, and a guy I know told me the birds are amazing. They wear long sort of floating dresses and go barefoot,' he added, with a sigh of pleasure.

Julie thought that the sentence suited Chris, with his faun's face and slanting eyes, and his air of being a creature about to vanish into the forest in pursuit of some flying girl . . .

Two weeks went by. They established a pattern. Every morning Julie worked with Robert Waring, starting immediately after breakfast and staying with him for as much as five hours.

It was an extraordinary experience, and Julie felt it was something she could describe to nobody. It was a sort of secret. He went through *Saint Joan* with her, he talked to her, opened his mind to her, and asked her many questions. He described the part, the girl and her enormous strengths, the tragedy and the comedy too; Joan's innocence and power as a woman of action, a genius in war, a virgin. But Robert Waring described other things that were not about Joan but about Julie. He told her, and he repeated it, that she must use her imagination stretched to its uttermost, that there was no limit to what she must make herself feel, and be, and think, and become in acting. She would come to a freedom in acting some day, but at present it would be all discipline and dedicated work. And then, with her imagination and talent, she'd develop the right sort of inspiration. He promised her this would be so.

He sat beside her and talked to her sometimes with fire and sometimes gently. She found him infinitely fascinating; she let herself be persuaded, wooed, taught and moulded. His manner was changeable but the doctrine he preached was not. She must use her imagination and her thoughts; she must work and think . . . and finally, trust to her instinct.

It was during this time, and it was not a small thing to her, that he told her she must cut her hair. He showed her the stage directions in *Saint Joan*, which described the saint with her hair 'bobbed and hanging round her face.'

'I want yours shorter than that. I want it jagged and short, like a boy's, like a soldier's,' Robert Waring said, and for a moment he picked up a long strand of Julie's hair and looked down at it.

And Julie thought : I think he's sorry that I must cut it off.

She made an appointment with the hairdresser he chose, a smart Greek hairdresser, young and rather arrogant, whom Julie had never visited before. One afternoon Julie returned to the Hampstead house looking a different girl.

She did not see Robert Waring until the next morning when they met after breakfast for their session of work. He came into the room quickly, and then stopped and looked at her.

'Yes,' he said. 'There is the Maid; with her mission from heaven.'

Julie knew he was pleased.

In the afternoons, when Robert Waring was gone to the Royalty or the film studios, Julie was left to her own devices. She would wander into the garden to think about Joan, or talk to Harriet in the kitchen, or walk on Hampstead Heath with Sheba, or take a taxi down to the West End and have tea with Chris. Now and again she went to the Turkish baths. Harriet encouraged these, not only because they helped with the diet, but also because Julie was often worn out with work and a Turkish bath helped her relax.

Julie had never had a Turkish bath until now; she soon became accustomed to sitting in the elegant steamy rooms, wrapped in enormous white towels, thinking of nothing but Joan, Joan.

One afternoon she was leaning against the steamy wall in a corner of one of the rooms, the steam floating round her as if she were in the crater of a volcano, while she slowly massaged cream into her cheeks. She did not feel relaxed this afternoon, she felt melancholy. On the way here she'd noticed a poster for the new production *Half in Half*, an eye-catching poster showing a man and a woman's profile, shattered like a reflection in a mirror. There was Tam's name; and David Bryden's name. And Daniel's. 'Sets and costumes by Daniel Monteith.'

Julie, rubbing the cream into her cheeks, thought: 'How stupid that even a name on a poster can hurt.'

'Why, Julie!' exclaimed a lively voice. Looming out of the clouds came Tam. Her red hair was dark copper with sweat. She was holding her towel with both hands. A tall fair girl with a starry, innocent face accompanied her.

'Harriet said we'd find you here, crouching behind a marble pillar like an old Roman senator,' said Tam. 'This is my sister Candida, by the way. Candida – this is Sir's new young lady!'

Julie was startled at just how beautiful this elder sister of Tam's turned out to be. She had seen her in films, of course. Close to, Candida was a sort of goddess.

'It's lovely to meet you at last,' Candida said. 'Tam and Harry keep talking about you and so does my father. How are you getting on? We do feel for you, you know. When we first played, Tam and I both had the same kind of treatment from Dad . . . all that dedicated work and worry. I'm sure you need lots of vitamins, love and support,' she added, smiling.

Candida sat beside Julie and Tam sat on the other side. The steam billowed round them. Dressed in flowing white, they were like three virgins in ancient Rome.

'Candy had exactly the same kind of time you are having,' said Tam. 'So did I, later on; so we're feeling rather *sisterly* about you just now, Julie. We hope you're keeping up your courage. He only gives you the real treatment once, you know, in a concentrated form, when you're beginning. After that, when it has worked for you, he leaves you much more on your own.'

Tam said this with the confident belief that, like her elder sister and herself, Julie would want to learn from Sir and then break free of him. But Julie wasn't sure. The prospect of Joan, the size and depth of the part, frightened her; so did the feeling that Sir expected so much. But the idea of being without him, without the support of his genius and his strength, was more alarming still.

She murmured something polite which really said nothing,

85

and Candida, quicker than Tam at intuitive things, pushed back a strand of damp fair hair and said, 'Dad may not do that with Julie. Push her out on her own, like he did with us. Maybe he'll sign her up at the Royalty with a line of parts next season and go on working with her.'

'And *at* her,' said Tam.

'That, too,' admitted Candida. 'Maybe you'd prefer that, Julie?'

'But why didn't you both take on a line of parts when you both had such successes? Didn't you want to stay with him?' Julie asked. It was something about both the Waring girls that always intrigued her.

'Oh, Tam made a movie,' Candida said, with her rather tremulous smile, 'and I went off and got married and had a baby. Dad wasn't best pleased about that. He's wild about Matthew now, of course, but at the time he was horrified at being a grandfather.'

'Yes, it *is* odd to think of him like that,' Julie said.

The sisters exchanged a brief look through the steam, and said nothing.

After the Turkish bath the girls had tea, and then the Warings saw Julie into her taxi and waved her goodbye.

When the car had driven off into the traffic, Candida asked Tam where she was going now.

'Nowhere special,' Tam said. 'David's working with Dan, and our run-through isn't for two hours. I feel jumpy. Shall we walk?'

'I was going to suggest the same thing,' Candida said. She knew her little sister and remembered that walking always soothed Tam.

'Let's walk to the National Gallery,' Candida said, 'and just look at *one* picture and then walk back to Dad's club.'

'Can I choose which picture?' was Tam's typical reply.

The girls had the Waring trick of communicating without words; they walked up Berkeley Square in the latening sunlight in silence.

It was Candida who finally spoke. 'She's very sweet-looking,' she said thoughtfully.

'Her face is too round for her to be really beautiful but she's lost a lot of weight. She's beginning to look as if her eyes are enormous. It's rather good, that look,' said Tam. 'She's a nice girl, Candy. One always knows when one shares a dressing-room; that's when the cats show their claws. Julie is a dear girl.'

'Dad thinks she's a find.'

'*I* thought so when she played Hero. But if Dad says so, then it's gospel.'

Candida smiled to herself. Her younger sister's awestruck attitude to her father still amused her.

Candida said, 'Don't you think she's a bit . . . subdued, Tam? I mean, she's only about twenty. Is Dad treating her well? You and I have known him all our lives. *We* know how to cope with him and when not to take him seriously. Even you stand up for yourself when necessary. But that girl looks so young and vulnerable. Like a deer.'

'Harry says *Dad* is being a cooing dove, mixing the similes,' said Tam cheerfully. 'I rang Harry yesterday and asked how the wind was blowing in Hampstead, and she said "distinctly southerly".'

'While he's working? That doesn't sound like Dad.'

'That's what I thought.'

They walked together through the sunlit streets, and arrived at the steps of the National Gallery.

'Let's go and pay our respects to the Velasquez,' suggested Candida.

It was the painting that had always reminded the girls of their father; they'd visited it often before. They walked into the great rooms which were emptying of visitors just before closing time, passed through galleries they'd known since they were children, and came to the painting. It stared at them, mocking, heroic, from the heavy gold frame.

'Tam . . .' murmured Candida, facing the portrait, her dreamy face very thoughtful indeed.

'Mm?'

'You don't actually think . . .'

Tam glanced at her and giggled. 'Oh yes I do,' Tam said.

'That Dad actually feels . . .'

'Go on. Say it.'

Candida said, 'With that face staring at me, it's difficult to actually say it. Sir is such a tyrant, he always has been, in a way it *suits* him to be king of the castle. He's a genius, too; that is what he is. And one we've lived with all our lives. So is it possible that *Dad* has begun to have softer feelings for that little girl we just saw wearing a bathrobe?'

'That's what Harry thinks,' Tam said. 'And just tell me, Candy, when is Harry ever wrong?'

Unaware that she was being talked about, unconscious of

having any effect on the Waring girls, Julie drove home in the taxi, staring out of the window at the flowering trees of early London summer. She thought : In a few days now I'll be at Condaford, miles away in the country. Life will be at a different pace, and then she added to herself : I won't be in the same city as Daniel any more.

Daniel. She still thought about him, however hard she tried not to. All the time she'd been working at the Hampstead house, every moment when she wasn't deeply involved and concentrated on *Saint Joan*, Daniel was somewhere in her mind, a reason for sadness and longing. Oh, but why? They had met briefly and liked each other and been happy in each other's company for a time . . . such a little time. And once they'd kissed. She remembered the kiss with wonder and pain. The wood had seemed quiet except for birdsong and the sound of the river, and quite suddenly Daniel had put his arms round her. Julie thought : All over this huge city, people are kissing like that. They're doing it now. People who scarcely know each other, who meet at parties, casually at parties. Like that big Australian boy the other day and the girl he was with. They laugh and dance a bit and kiss just like Daniel and me. You feel so close and it's so beautiful and it seems important and it isn't. That's all that happened between Daniel and me. Why do I feel so sad, so sad?

It must be because Daniel had thrown her over after Sir had made her the great offer. How could one *like* a man who did such a thing? It was all the worse because she'd thought Daniel was a man who looked on women as his equal; she'd never sensed the least tang of that man-versus-woman thing that would make him reject a girl because she was talented, ambitious even . . .

She wondered, for the hundredth time, if there could be another less hurtful reason why Daniel had deserted her. Did he dislike Sir Robert? How could that be true, he scarcely knew him. Had he thought it undignified, an affront to male dignity to be put off by Julie that evening when Sir first offered her Joan? That was not true either, for when Julie remembered Daniel's strong face, he wasn't a man to be 'affronted'. He was confident, easy and kind. Except to me, she thought, and tears came into her eyes.

It was quiet when she got back to the Hampstead house. The telephone didn't ring; Sir Robert's secretary had gone home; there was no sign of Harriet; no sight or sound of Sir.

Relieved by the peace and silence, Julie fetched her copy of *Saint Joan* and walked out into the garden.

Seated on the terrace in the late sunshine, accompanied by a dozing Sheba, was a middle-aged man. He was short and thin, with straight white hair and a pink face. He was reading a pink newspaper to match (it was the *Financial Times*). Julie guessed this must be Sir Robert's financier friend, Renfred de Buisson.

He saw Julie, stood up and bowed. 'Miss Woods, of course.'

He took her hand and kissed it. 'Renfred de Buisson. Bobby has told me all about you. A pleasure, Miss Woods.'

Julie had not been looking forward to the arrival of a stranger in the house; when she remembered it, she had almost dreaded his coming as a distraction and an interruption. Sir had said Renfred liked women; he had omitted to add that women loved Renfred. To any woman he was irresistible. He was quiet and relaxed, amused and kind, polite and acute; so French and so Hungarian. 'I am half in half, like David Bryden's play,' he said to Julie. 'You will find that I am full of both country's prejudices!'

He spoke English with no accent except the slight drawl you might hear in a man who belonged to a classy regiment; the Guards, perhaps. He was fiftyish, his skin clear and rosy, his eyes shrewd and faded blue. He was gentle. Julie thought this must be a deceptive impression, for Sir had told her de Buisson was a millionaire and the shrewdest operator in films he had ever met.

'How's *Joan* going? The casting sounded hopeful, I thought. How are the rehearsals?' Renfred asked.

'Still a bit uncertain. Not set. Sort of rough and ready,' Julie admitted.

'It won't set until the day before it opens,' Renfred said sympathetically. 'Bobby likes to keep things fluid during the rehearsal period. It's something I noticed about him years ago. When he finally does set it, he keeps it like that down to the last detail. He's a martinet as well as an artist. Have you done your big scenes with him yet?'

'No. He only mutters through them.'

'The fire will come later,' Renfred said, smiling. 'He plays the Inquisitor, doesn't he? That huge speech. A hundred and fifty-three lines if I remember right.'

'You know Shaw very well.'

'I know Bobby very well,' was the reply.

They lingered in the garden as the sun went down. She liked being with this man, with his drawling voice and faded eyes.

'I'm producing a motion picture in the autumn, and I've managed to get Bobby to play in it,' he observed. 'I dare say he's told you about it? It's a peach of a part. Like the Inquisitor in *Joan* it comes in at the end of the show like a great roll of drums with a hundred and fifty-three lines to follow. He'll be great. I'm feeling good about the movie just now. Keeping my fingers crossed, of course, so many bad things can happen so quickly! But at present I've signed most of the actors in the main parts, and the cast is good. The location – near Rio de Janiero – is glorious. And I've just fixed for a first-class designer. Talking about designers,' he added, 'who is doing *Joan*?'

'A woman called Beatrice Lang. I haven't met her yet.'

'Beatrice,' he said. 'That's odd.'

'Why? Don't you like her work?' enquired Julie.

'Very much. She's the one who has just begun working on my pictures.'

Julie was horrified. Had she given away one of Sir's professional secrets? She went scarlet, and laughed in the self-conscious way of someone who is out of countenance.

'Perhaps I've got the name wrong. I must have done,' she said in an embarrassed voice.

Renfred de Buisson was not in the least embarrassed. He retained his bland, pink-faced serenity.

'I dare say Bobby's up to one of his conjuring tricks,' he said. 'That's nothing new. I told him weeks ago I was planning on Beatrice, and I remember thinking he was very interested. It's nothing new, and nothing to worry about, Miss Woods. One thing I am sure of is that you haven't got your facts wrong!'

There was a pause. Renfred de Buisson was silent, looking rather thoughtful as he gazed at the shadowy garden. Julie, the play unopened in her lap, found herself thinking how exhausting it was to live in an atmosphere of what Chris called 'the big marbles.' The loss of a designer, an actor, a play, could mean thousands . . . many thousands of pounds. Sometimes she was homesick for Rep and Chris and steak and chips.

Renfred de Buisson roused himself from his reverie and said, 'The man Bobby needs for *Saint Joan* is that clever newcomer, Daniel Monteith.'

At the sound of Daniel's name Julie felt rather sick. It was stupid, she knew, but she could do nothing about these miserable feelings of hers. She did not reply, and her companion continued, 'You probably know Monteith's work as he's doing Tam's new play. To my mind, he's one of the best of the new lot. Beatrice's work is far too detailed and scholarly for *Joan* . . . she'd spend her time researching on the armour and the pennants! She's right for my South American motion picture, but much too elaborate for Shaw – and such a Shaw. A masterpiece. Bobby really ought to get hold of Monteith. We'll tell him at supper-time.'

Julie smiled and wished devoutly that she could be out at 'supper-time' as he called it.

Dinner was to be rather late that evening; Sir Robert was at the TV Centre, in an interview about State subsidies for the arts – a subject he spoke about with some energy.

When Julie went upstairs to change, she decided she would wear a new dress. It was rather a particular dress, the first that Sir had ever chosen for her. He'd seen it on a drive to the theatre and suggested she should go and have a look at it. Julie had gone, the same day, and bought it.

But she hadn't worn it until now. It would perhaps, she thought, cheer her up while Daniel was being discussed during the meal.

It was the oddest dress and in the dullest colours, Julie thought, looking at herself in the long glass in the bathroom. The browns were pinkish, the pinks were greyish, the blues were slatey, the greens had a yellow tinge dimming into grey. It was long and simple, and its design was geometric, like Greek or Cretan patterns. There were lines and squares and angles blending into each other. It was as if she were wearing something painted by an artist thousands of years ago, a design faded by the sun and by time.

Yet when she wore it, it enhanced her.

Renfred and Sir were in the drawing-room as she came into the room. Actor and financier turned to look at her and Julie thought : The dress works.

As she came towards them, Sir Robert said : 'Well? What do you think of her, Renfred? Does she come up to expectations, mmm?' He took her by the left hand and turned her to and fro as one might do to a child.

'Quite the work of art,' said Renfred, and Julie thought he was laughing at his friend's pride in her; but perhaps she was wrong.

91

'She's not a work of art yet but give me time,' said Robert Waring. 'Julie, pour yourself out a glass of Perrier. And Renfred informs me that you've let my cat out of the bag with a vengeance. Can't you keep my secrets?'

'Always. When you tell me they are secrets.'

'How frank the young are,' he said, sighing. 'Nothing gets veiled or wrapped up; where's the disguise? Very well, I admit I didn't tell you to keep mum about Beatrice. I haven't decided to give her up, I might add.'

'She'll do scrappy work if you insist on keeping her,' remarked Renfred, finishing his drink. 'She'll stick to her contract with you because she's a nice creature with what in Hungary we call "a heart of honour". But no amount of honourable heart can make Bee do good work on two productions at the same time. Remember when she did the Pinero and *Twelfth Night*? Poor Beatrice simply fell to pieces.'

'She is in perfectly satisfactory shape now,' remarked Sir Robert, rather as if he were speaking about a vase.

'And you think you'll keep her like that with your famous persuasive quality?' said Renfred.

Julie thought his tone of voice downright worrying. It was so sure.

Apparently Robert Waring thought the same. 'What have you got up your sleeve, Renfred?'

'Not much. Only Beatrice's ideas for the picture . . .'

The conversation lapsed.

During dinner Harriet and Julie were quiet, and the men did most of the talking. As Julie had expected, the matter of Beatrice soon came up again, and this time – so did Daniel's name.

'I must say I don't understand why you have not considered Daniel Monteith as your designer for *Joan*. He's very talented,' said Renfred. 'Do you know his work, Bobby? Harriet?'

'I saw a Beckett season he designed. Glass and cloud and reflections – the actors seeming in space. Rather beautiful, as a matter of fact,' Harriet said.

'Now why are you asking *Harry*'s opinion of design?' exclaimed Robert Waring impatiently. 'If Harry's truthful, all she's interested in is the ballet. We don't want *Joan* looking like *Lac de Cygnes*, do we?'

Harriet continued to eat peacefully.

'What do you think of him yourself?' pursued Renfred, not to be put off. 'You'll admit he's clever.'

'Clever is not enough. He's a bit cheap. Arresting, yes, but lacking scholarship.'

'Why should you need that!' exclaimed Renfred, with more energy than Julie had heard him use before. 'The man's an artist, not a don. An instinctive artist, who uses today's materials to get extraordinary effects. He's not just a theatre historian. I need Beatrice to provide costumes for an old-scale South American epic where every horse's saddle must be right. You know the kind of thing only too well. But *you're* working with a masterpiece.'

'I thought the Beckett designs tiresome,' drawled Robert Waring.

The meal was ended, and Julie and Harriet were eating walnuts, which Harriet was cracking neatly and passing to Julie, rather like an elder sister at Christmas dinner.

Suddenly her brother exploded.

'Do stop making that infernal din, Harry! I feel as if you had my nerves in that nutcracker!'

'I'm so sorry,' she said, not in the least put out. 'Perhaps Julie and I could finish them in the kitchen. They're very delicious.'

'Finish your meal in the kitchen because I forbid you to deafen me by cracking nuts!' cried Robert Waring. 'What next? Where was I, Renfred? The women have made me forget my train of thought.'

'They do, don't they?' said Renfred approvingly. 'We were discussing Monteith as a replacement for Beatrice. What about him? Consider him, anyway. Tam rang to say she was coming round for coffee, and I took the liberty of asking her to bring some of Monteith's designs if she can find any in the house.'

Sir Robert reacted irritably. Renfred, he said, was an old operator; a Wall Street gnome. He had no right to meddle in theatre affairs and teach his *grandson* to suck eggs. 'You stick to what you do brilliantly,' he finished. 'And that is signing cheques!'

Renfred appeared to enjoy the scolding, and as the meal was ended and Julie and Harriet were allowed no more walnuts, they went into the drawing-room for coffee.

Music was playing as Harriet and Julie sat down, Renfred and Sir Robert lit the small cheroots which they both enjoyed. Julie heard the ring of the front door bell, and a moment

93

later the sound of Tam's laugh.

And then, quite suddenly, she *knew* Daniel was in the house. She could tell that he was near her and that she was going to see him. She froze, watching the door.

It opened, and Tamara and David came in, smiling. Following them, looking somehow taller and older than in her imagination, came Daniel.

The record player was filling the room with tinkling heartless music; the place was full of flowers and low lights and the pungent smell of cigars and the chatter of greeting. Tam hugged her father, and Julie looked over at Daniel and thought, eager, anxious : are we going to greet each other as friends?

He saw her in the room's rich setting, wearing the strange-coloured dress. She was much thinner than he remembered; her face, with the eyes enlarged and the cheekbones shadowed, was a kind of shock. So was her short jagged hair in place of the long soft curling hair that had fallen about her shoulders.

He bowed slightly.

Sir Robert was the soul of welcome. He bustled about, pouring drinks and making his guests comfortable. Renfred and Tam, who'd been fond of each other for years, sat together and talked. Robert Waring and his son-in-law began a conversation. Harriet went quietly out of the room in search of fresh coffee. And Julie was near Daniel.

'May I get you a drink?' she said, sounding as tinkling and heartless, she thought, as the music.

'A glass of wine if you have it.' He was perfectly polite.

'I don't know what we've got . . . I'll go and see.' She went over to the drinks table and poured him a glass of white wine.

'Aren't you drinking, too?' he said, looking down at her. He was so tall, he seemed to loom.

'Sir won't let me. I'm on a fearsome diet. It's a great strain on my willpower.' She thought : How stupid I sound.

'I'm sure,' he answered.

And she knew, by his polite, indifferent voice and everything he didn't say, that he had not forgiven her.

Robert Waring came across the room just then, and by some sorcery of his own succeeded in bringing the attention on to himself. Everyone in the room turned to look at him, although he addressed his remarks to Daniel.

'Renfred has been raving about your work to me all day; your ears must have been on fire,' he added, raising his eyebrows and giving Daniel such a smile. It was brilliant; it gleamed; it reminded Julie of some great jungle creature, a leopard perhaps. She felt quite nervous for Daniel facing such an opponent.

'Renfred says the Royalty would be out of their minds not to capture you before you go off to Hollywood to design films or before another rival theatre gets you,' continued Sir Robert. 'You've already used your marvellous talent on Beckett. And now – with my daughter Tamara – ' he gave a graceful gesture towards Tam who seemed pleased and touched.

(Hypocrite! thought Julie. Don't believe him, Daniel!)

'So we have been wondering,' continued Sir Robert smoothly, 'what you would think about designing *Saint Joan*.'

Julie had the oddest feeling, watching this scene. She no longer felt involved with her own play – she just wanted Daniel to refuse. She'd been in the thrall of Sir, a girl imprisoned by a sorcerer, for weeks, and now she was awake, shaking herself, seeing him as Tam sometimes described him.

'May I hope you like the idea?' said Robert Waring.

'Very much indeed, sir. I am honoured. More than honoured. I only wish that I could accept.'

A frisson ran through the room like a breeze through rushes.

'Not accept, my dear fellow? Of course you must accept,' said Sir Robert. 'Or are you signed up with someone else?' he added, rather too sharply, and Renfred laughed.

'No, Sir Robert, I am not. But David's play doesn't open for ten days, and surely you want . . .'

'For you to start work at once? True. However, the best artists usually manage to do two things at the same time. I often do myself,' said Sir Robert, looking with veiled eyes across at Renfred. 'You could surely begin preliminary work on *Joan* before you complete *Half in Half*? Do you agree, David, my boy?'

'The main work for *Half* is complete, Dan,' David said, leaning forwards. How differently David looks at him, thought Julie, from the way Sir Robert does! David's attitude to Daniel was that of a man who was truly fond of him and admired him and wished him well; he wasn't a hungry panther planning to eat Daniel for tomorrow's lunch.

'It's a terrific chance to design for Condaford,' David was saying generously. 'You *must* take it. I'm sure we can manage with so little left to do for *Half*. It's the chance of a lifetime

95

for you to work with Sir.'

'I agree,' said Sir Robert.

Daniel laughed and Julie thought : I believe Sir amuses him. He made a graceful speech and he and Robert Waring moved out of the general conversation together, and out of the scene created by the star for his own purpose.

Julie did not speak to Daniel again until it was time for the guests to go. Sir Robert had been called – inevitably – away to the telephone. Daniel was sitting on the arm of the settee, listening to the talk but taking no part in it.

She went over to him.

He stood up and she thought : He won't even pay me the friendly compliment of remaining relaxed.

'Do sit, Daniel,' she said, needing an effort to sound natural. 'I only came over to say how glad I am about your news. It's wonderful that you're designing *Saint Joan*.'

The others were talking and laughing, and Daniel, looming over Julie and speaking in a cool voice, said, 'But Sir had already signed Beatrice Lang. So why the sudden switch?'

She was taken aback and said nothing.

He looked down at her for a moment. She looked very small and thin and he disliked the jagged hair.

'Come now, Julie,' he said with a cold smile, 'I trust you haven't been playing fairy godmother. That would be a mistake in the circumstances, wouldn't it?'

She didn't understand and her face showed it.

He was impatient at the earnest expression.

'I mean,' he said sourly, 'that I am aware of just how much flattery was used just now. He spread it like butter. He did not need to spread the butter quite so thick for me, you know. Any designer in his right mind would jump at the chance.'

'He wasn't laying it on thick,' she said sharply.

Daniel upset her, and her loyalty to Robert Waring at once revived.

'Oh, I'm sorry. I quite forgot to whom I was speaking,' he said derisively, and the tone of his voice was an actual shock.

They stared at each other, and at that moment Robert Waring came back into the room.

It was time for the guests to go. Harriet and Robert Waring saw them off, kissed them goodbye, accompanied them to the door hospitably.

Julie and Renfred stayed alone in the drawing-room. Renfred, smoking a second cheroot, looked at her for a moment but said nothing.

Robert Waring came back into the drawing-room with a springing step. He looked cheerful and as fresh as an early morning.

'Well, little Joan,' he said, coming over to her and taking her hands. 'You'll have a clever designer working for you. That'll make you happy!'

4

The uneven-shaped room had been used to store apples once upon a time. It still had a rustic character, as if wisps of hay might perhaps be discovered on top of the wardrobe. The floor, of large stone flags, looked like grey silk through age and varnish, and beams branched across whitewashed walls. One water colour, a costume design of a helmeted figure wearing a crimson cloak, hung near Julie's divan bed.

She had pushed her desk up close to the french window and piled it with books; every day Julie seemed to collect another volume about the Middle Ages or Saint Joan. She studied them for hours, never glancing into the garden at the strip of lawn which sloped down to an overgrown stream.

Julie had been in Condaford a week now and felt settled. Her home was ideal for a busy actress; it was unconventional and easy, very quiet, not over-furnished but attractive. Apart from the picture on the wall, the few things about the place were her own. Her small apartment was to be an empty canvas for her Condaford life.

Moving the Royalty's second company from London to Condaford had been like organizing the progress of an army. There were sixty actors and their families; there were also all the people, skilful and highly trained, whom the public never remembered but whose work made up the drama's essence : directors and assistants, publicity and publications staff, stage management, property and wardrobe people, lighting experts, electricians, a great army of the Arts. The army had descended on Condaford, occupying houses and cottages, flats and mews dwellings, caravans – even house boats. The overworked Royalty management brought the move about efficiently and were now coping with justified and unjustified demands (usually from the actors); one of the most usual was the plaintive : 'My wife wants to know which half of the garden is ours.'

Julie had been spared the worry and exhaustion of the move. She'd asked Harriet weeks ago when she ought to go down to Condaford and see about digs. Harriet had said, 'Sir's fixing it. He doesn't want you bothered.' Julie felt delicious guilty relief. Packing up on the last morning before leaving Hampstead, she thought : So this is how stars feel! No midday trains had to be caught, with changes and waits on deserted stations; no lifts were kindly given in cars piled so high with other actors and their luggage that one small Rep actress spent the journey perched on a stranger's knee, her head against the car roof; no frantic rush at journey's end was necessary to find a home – any home – on the 'list of possibles' dished out by the Rep's stage manager.

Bound for Condaford, Julie simply stepped into Sir's car and enjoyed a long, fast drive to the country. And that was that.

She had no idea where she was going to live, and when she asked Sir during the drive, he said airily, 'I think you'll find it to your liking. Candida stayed there when she was playing *Twelfth Night*. She assures me the place has good vibrations.'

Julie, studying him under her eyelashes, decided his face was distinctly gleeful; she wondered what he was up to.

'I'm looking forward to seeing my new home; it is good of everybody to fix it for me. It's usually such a worry and a scramble . . .'

'We must take good care of you, Julie.'

Did she amuse him, Julie wondered? It was pretty obvious that she did. But hadn't that been a slightly tender glance Sir shot at her before looking back at the road? They were driving alone; now and again Sir gave his chauffeur some deserved time off. Thinking about the look, which Julie had seen once or twice before on Robert Waring's face, she decided it was probably the look of a painter selecting a tube of paint. The idea that she was a medium for his art, and not an attractive woman, put her on her mettle to *have* an effect on him.

'It'll be odd . . . not being with you any more . . .' she murmured.

A pause.

'I shall miss you,' Julie added, light as a feather.

'Somehow,' he remarked, looking at her drolly, 'I don't think you will.'

He burst out laughing and Julie thought: Now where's the joke?

When Robert Waring had previously worked at Condaford, during the successful seasons at the drama and arts festival, he had lived at Ravenfield. This was an early nineteenth-century house four miles outside the town, and had belonged to the Condaford Trust for many years. It was used as a kind of local Ten Downing Street for the year's most important visitor. And Sir, of course, was given Ravenfield again this year.

The house was long and low, painted white, looking very like a Regency painting of a 'minor manor house'. It stood in large gardens well hidden from the road by trees and an old brick wall. The original owner in the 1820s had created it when he returned from India, it was a copy of his residence there; Ravenfield had verandas and terraces all round the house. The effect was stately. So was the curved drive, walled kitchen garden, stone urns trailing with ivy. For 150 years Ravenfield had kept its Regency grace.

Not so the outhouses, servants' quarters, dairies, stables, apple lofts, gardeners' cottages and a couple of garages. These had been converted into a rabbit warren of dwellings of various sizes and were let to actors and theatre staff working at the festival.

Ravenfield represented two worlds, connected but divided. Sir Robert strolled on his fine lawns or sat on his terrace, working in the sunshine. But behind hedges and walls, upstairs and down, numerous other Royalty people lived and worked, and wisely kept to their part of the gardens.

Julie's flat was one of the converted outhouses, built to the side of the 'Big House', as people called the main building. When she and Sir Robert arrived at Ravenfield, he walked with her across a stableyard and threw open the door of her small flat with a flourish.

'Now I'll show you something interesting,' he said, opening the french windows on to the little garden, which had high hedges on either side of it. He pointed to the hedge on the left.

'*I'm* on the other side of *that*!'

Julie finally understood the joke.

In the week that followed she didn't have time to decide
whether or not she liked being so close to the big house and
the big star. She scarcely had time to unpack her clothes, hang
them in the cupboards where the apples had been stored, and
discover the village shops. The Royalty's music director, who
also had a Ravenfield flat, called for her and drove her to
rehearsal before she'd been in her home half an hour.

Hasty shopping, whole days of rehearsal, snatched meals,
meetings with Sir at the big house, that was the way it had
been for a week. Julie hadn't once sat down in her own strip
of garden.

But today was Sunday. Robert Waring had informed his
Company the previous evening that they could have Sunday
off.

There had been a murmur of pleasure.

'Until six sharp,' he'd added sweetly.

Since the day the Company arrived at Condaford, the
weather had been exquisite. Today was again beautiful, warm
but not hot, rather still, with a sound of cooing wood pigeons.
Julie's french window stood open, and as she looked down the
narrow little garden she saw that a willow, bent over the
stream, was covered with a lemon-green mist of leaves.

She took some cushions and went barefoot into the garden
to sunbathe, wearing lilac shorts and an old white T shirt.
She flopped on the grass and stared up at the sky, listening to
the pigeons' summer sound.

She thought : Peace.

But work teased her as she lay in the sunshine. Yesterday
she'd played a scene with Robert Waring when, for the first
time he had *acted* instead of just speaking the lines while
directing other players. He'd lounged over to Julie, wearing
his denim working suit and looking full of sparkle and energy,
and said, 'Let us do this little duet.'

As they took their places facing each other, Robert Waring
changed in some extraordinary way. He seemed to shrink
and wither; he was a soft-voiced old man, a man of the
Church – and of stone. He was implacable.

Julie was suddenly desperately nervous and when she
replied, she stuttered. The scene ended, and Robert Waring
moved out of it like a skater stepping off the ice. He said :
'Keep the stutter. It works.'

Now, sitting in the garden alone, Julie thought of Robert

Waring. She didn't think of him as her familiar friend, the quirky, autocratic starry companion who had given her such an astonishing chance to play Saint Joan, or who was every day teaching her more about how to do it. She didn't think of him as the head of the Royalty, the man they deferred to, the man who made everything happen. She just saw him as the marvellous actor . . .

'Anybody at home?' called a loud cheerful voice, and turning round she saw Chris framed in the window in the sun.

'Come and join me,' Julie said. 'It's lovely in the garden after being indoors for so long.'

'I can't believe he's actually given us a bit of time off,' said Chris, stepping over to her.

He sat down on the grass by Julie and rummaged in a bulging orange-coloured carrier bag.

'I've brought us a bottle,' he said. 'Hey, I forgot, you can't drink. Ah well, then I brought *me* a bottle. I suppose the old Demon will allow you to eat a strawberry or two? I got this little punnet down the road.'

Chris picked out a large dry strawberry and popped it into her mouth.

'Dan Monteith and Clover arrived last night. Did Sir tell you Daniel is going to live in the laundry flat? And Clover's staying with the music director Rufus and his wife. So you'll all be neighbours.'

'I didn't know Daniel was at Ravenfield,' Julie said after a moment's silence.

'They always give the laundry flat to the designer,' said Chris, with his little air of having known Condaford practice for years instead of days. 'As you'll have guessed, it was where the big house had all its washing and ironing done. The laundry flat has a huge workroom which is handy as Dan and Clover apparently arrived with mounds of stuff. Files and card indexes and drawing boards and things, and huge books of photographs, and boxes of fabric samples, and about five model sets . . . amazing! I remember when I called at Dan's London studio, I was dead impressed with all his materials.'

He picked out some more strawberries and said, 'You'll enjoy Dan at Ravenfield, Julie. You rather fancied him when we were at the Sheridan, I remember.'

'Did I?'

'Oh, you old poker face,' he said, laughing. 'Where's my

mate who used to tell me her secrets? You certainly *did* fancy
Dan Monteith, and if you've now stopped we must take it
that's because you have your greedy eye fixed in far more
exalted spheres!'

'Chris, don't be stupid.'

'Want to be Her Ladyship?' said Chris, and laughed so
much that he rolled over on the grass and upset the strawberries.

He stayed to lunch, hard-boiled eggs and lettuce served in
the garden, and left, with groans, for the theatre, to work in
the afternoon.

Julie returned to the cushions on the lawn and sunbathing
and her thoughts. Daniel was here and she had better get
used to it. She must not become upset during this all-import-
ant period of rehearsal, just when she felt it was beginning to
happen for her. It *was* beginning to run, the play was beginning to run like music, like starting a new life. She sometimes
felt she was actually inside the skin of the assertive, rustic,
inexperienced, inspired girl called Joan of Arc.

Nothing must distract her now.

So, she must get herself used to seeing Daniel and his
Clover (whom she'd never met), and to working with both of
them. She and Daniel would need to meet because the designer worked with the director and the actors as part of the
team. It would be important to work with Daniel and she
must accept it. She must stop feeling hurt when she spoke of
him momentarily or even when somebody said his name.

Her meeting with him was sooner than she expected. Later
in the afternoon she left her front door open and went out
into the sunny stableyard to see if she could find Rufus to ask
if he could give her a lift to the theatre. The first person
she saw was Daniel.

His open car was parked by a wall which was covered in
honeysuckle, and Daniel was standing in conversation with a
girl. He looked very tall and relaxed, in a white shirt with
short sleeves and dark blue trousers; he looked as if he'd been
living here for years. The girl beside him was rather small,
with long black hair and a round pale face. She wore large
owl-like glasses; Julie guessed she must be Clover.

Daniel saw Julie immediately, as if he were expecting to do
so. He walked over to her.

'Hallo, Daniel,' she said cheerfully. 'Chris tells me we are
neighbours and that you're moving in today.'

'Yes. We arrived late last night,' he said pleasantly. 'We're all unpacked now but it was quite a job. May I introduce you to Clover? She's been looking forward to meeting you.'

'How do you do,' said Clover, coming across the yard eagerly, and taking Julie's hand. 'It's great to meet you. Dan's already started on your *Joan* designs . . . they are going to be marvellous!'

Daniel said indulgently, 'You mustn't listen to Clover when she talks about work. I am always telling her she will have to stop being a fan.'

'But it must be good having someone with you who admires your work, surely? It must give you confidence,' Julie said politely.

Clover giggled. 'Dan doesn't take a blind bit of notice of what *I* say! He says I'm a solid mass of prejudice.'

The trio talked for a little longer and Julie felt relieved and depressed. It was exactly as it was supposed to be. Perfectly friendly and polite. But Daniel and Clover were united in the way they talked to each other. *She* was the outsider.

'Come and see the laundry flat,' Clover said to Julie. 'Rehearsal isn't for half an hour. Rufus is driving us in, he said he'd hoot when he's ready. We've got heaps of time,' she added, consulting a large gold watch which she wore pinned to her cotton blouse like a nurse. 'Let's show Julie the workshop, Dan.'

Daniel said of course, and they walked across the courtyard to a cottage not far from Julie's flat.

Julie had an idea that Daniel didn't want to take her into the workshop; or perhaps it was simply that he didn't want to talk to her much. But Clover was the link between them and it was Clover, chatting about designs, who made the awkward meeting work.

The laundry room was large and bright, the floor unstained, the furniture of plain wood, tables, benches and shelves like a carpenter's. On one high wall was pinned an orderly confusion of fascinating things . . . old posters, watercolours of costumes, postcards of church treasures, pieces of fabric, metal jewellery, charcoal drawings, a string of bracelets. On the largest table was a model of a stage set made of board and plywood, already set about with miniature furniture.

'Act One,' said Clover. 'That's the archway where Joan enters from the stableyard.'

Julie knelt on a chair and stared intently at the tiny miraculous world in which she . . . Joan . . . was going to exist. The room, a stone chamber in a castle, seemed full of sunlight. The mullioned window overlooked a distant view of hills; the view, small and exquisite as an illumination in a vellum book, was painted on a sheet and pinned on a frame behind the window.

'Dan researched about twenty French châteaux,' Clover said, 'and took endless photographs when he was over in France. Here are a few of them.' She showed Julie boxes of photographs of castles, taken from near and at a distance, close-ups of windows and doors, views of turrets, moats, dungeons, courtyards, assembly halls, crumbling walls, half-effaced carvings.

'But how could you possibly have the time!' exclaimed Julie to Daniel as she stood looking at photograph after photograph. 'Why, you only – '

'I've worked on *Joan of Arc* before,' he said. 'Last year when we did *Henry VI* which includes Shakespeare's *Joan*, as you know. The references are the same.'

'We couldn't have done this *Joan* if it hadn't been for the work we did last year,' said Clover. 'We were months getting it all together. I practically lived at the British Museum, and Dan was ages away in France. Now Dan knows the period so well that . . . I mean, he can tell you precisely what they wore and what they ate and what they fought with and . . .'

'And, Clover, you are running on,' interrupted Daniel.

'But I like it. It's helpful,' Julie said tactfully. 'Perhaps I could talk to you both about the historical background. I'd be glad to.'

'Sir Robert must have done that with you already,' Daniel said.

'Oh yes, but it's all *here*!' said Julie, as Clover opened a book of enormous blown-up photographs, showing wall hangings and tapestries of figures in armour, ladies in Court dress.

'That's going to be the basis of one of Joan's designs,' said Clover, pointing at a warrior in the centre of a group of horsemen.

'Clover, I don't want our leading actress to see the ideas before we've settled on them,' said Daniel decisively. 'Shut that book, there's a dear girl. And isn't that the car?'

Julie became accustomed to seeing Daniel around in Condaford, or meeting him in Ravenfield. Sometimes he would attend a rehearsal and sit listening or drawing, his long legs stretched in front of him. Sir Robert would be directing a scene, or showing an actor some particular point in playing, and Daniel would look up, and then down again at his sketch book.

Clover was much in evidence, making appointments for the actors' fittings, or darting about with her hands full of a variety of things, from rolls of silk to piles of old books. Now and again her round, earnest face was spattered with paint after a visit to the workshops.

One afternoon, during a rehearsal break, Julie was having coffee in the Green Room with one of the actors when Daniel came in. He came over to her and said, 'I was looking for you. Can you spare me a little time?'

'How long?' she answered, and noticed too late that she sounded brusque.

'About half an hour. Sir says he isn't starting again till then.'

They went out into the sunny afternoon. Julie was wearing her practice clothes, a pair of black cord trousers that had seen better days, a black sweater, and sandals. Sir Robert liked these clothes for the scenes when she was dressed as a soldier; she had to play the scenes wearing some old leather armour, to get used to the weight and unwieldiness. Now, driving with Daniel in the brilliant sunshine, she was suddenly conscious that she looked plain and shabby in her worn clothes, with jagged hair and shiny face. Daniel himself had a brown velvet jacket and looked as elegant as Sir himself.

It was quiet when they arrived back at Ravenfield. The big house and the gardens were deserted. There were no cars parked by the rose-beds, all the owners were at rehearsal.

Daniel opened the car door for Julie, and they crossed the yard in silence and went up the stairs to the laundry flat. They came into the huge workroom, where the litter of work was growing, more designs pinned up, more photographs, piles of fabric and props . . .

'No Clover today?' said Julie, breaking the silence.

'She's gone to London to get some fabric. It's for your Rheims costume, as a matter of fact,' Daniel said. 'This is the one.'

He picked up a design lying on the table. It was the first piece of Daniel's work on *Saint Joan* which Julie had seen and she looked down at it with a painful curiosity. Sir had once said to her: 'Know a man by his work, Julie. Me by mine. Joan of Arc by hers.' Julie remembered this as she looked at the bold, beautiful painting.

It was of a young girl, strangely like and unlike herself. The figure was in armour, wearing a white and gold surcoat, a golden breastplate, a leather belt with gold tassels slung round the hips. The jagged hair and a look of large eyes indicated that the wearer was Julie, though he had not done a portrait of her. The figure carried a heavy, chased sword.

'It's very fine,' Julie said at last.

'I hope it will be all right for you. Right for the scene,' he said gravely.

They stood looking at the drawing together.

'Your first fitting for the costume ought to be tomorrow,' he said. 'Clover will fix it, or one of the Wardrobe people. I really only wanted to show you this. And one or two preliminary things.'

He went over to a table and picked up a studded white armlet. He said 'May I?' and fitted it on to her arm, lacing it dexterously.

'It must support the wrist,' he said, 'but never be too tight. The sword is very heavy and a girl needs extra strength when it is swung in a fight . . . Joan was a great warrior and in the front of the battle . . . you need support here.' He fixed the laces differently, intent and frowning as he bent over her wrist.

As he stood close to her, Julie said suddenly, 'Daniel.'

'Mm?'

'What is the matter between you and me?'

The room, the house, the summer afternoon, was hushed. Daniel did not look up from fixing the armlet, and after a moment said, 'Is that more comfortable?'

'Yes. It's very comfortable and strong.' And she repeated, 'I said what has happened between us? Why are you annoyed with me, Daniel?'

She had forced him to look at her and he did it with a curious expression, as if – she thought – as if he didn't know her.

'Nothing is the matter, I hope,' he answered lightly. 'Now let me fix this collar. It's quite heavy.'

Julie tried to bring him back to the subject although he'd put her off coolly. She had nerved herself to speak about it and she wanted a frank reply. She repeated, 'But what happened between us, Daniel?'

All he did was to fetch a cape and fix it to her shoulders and ask her to try on a helmet. She was fascinated and distracted by the accoutrements of Saint Joan. The sword was heavy, the helmet had a floating plume. The collar round her neck weighed her down, but not as much as her anxious thoughts. Daniel ignored the second question and she knew she had to stop trying.

He replaced collar, helmet, armour, cape, laid the design on the table, ready for work. He drove Julie back to the theatre.

And it was only when he'd left her and she'd run through into the dark rehearsal room, already buzzing with waiting actors, that she knew how much Daniel had hurt her, and how much it was her fault for asking him to.

She'd only seen Robert Waring during working hours lately, and that night when rehearsal broke at last and she trailed out of the theatre with Chris, it was a little shock to hear a commanding voice calling, 'Julie!' from a large, waiting car.

'The old Demon's waiting, dammit,' muttered Chris. 'See you around, mate!'

'Hop in,' said Sir Robert. 'I thought we'd dine together. Am I taking you away from your friends?'

'Only Chris . . .' Julie murmured. The car moved off, and as usual she was surprised that the engine made no noise.

'The junior ASM?' said Robert Waring. 'I gather he's the one who's after all the girls.'

'He works hard,' said Julie sharply, and was answered by a guffaw.

It was nearly midnight and there was a moon. The Condaford tourist traffic was gone; the moon washed over the fields, turning them into ghostly lakes. When Sir Robert turned into the Ravenfield drive, Julie could smell night-scented flowers through the open car windows.

All the Ravenfield cars were parked by the rose-beds. The front door of the big house stood ajar, and as they went in, Sheba welcomed them with a thump of her tail.

'Harry's in bed,' Robert Waring said. 'There's food in the dining-room.'

In the dining-room, as stately as Sir Robert's own, a meal was laid, chicken mayonnaise and a peach salad. He put some food on two plates and led the way into the garden room. It was furnished with wicker chairs and settees, indoor plants and creepers, and opened on to the terrace.

'Harry always says that when one is tired, it's better to have a comfortable chair and eat on one's lap,' he said. 'Sit down, child.'

Julie sat meekly, the plate of food on her lap.

It was midnight and they had rehearsed all day. It was moonlight and they'd started just after the sun rose. He'd directed and coaxed and grumbled and exclaimed, he acted the Inquisitor and made that tremendous speech, he had ordered the Saint to her death. He was fresh and energetic and ate his supper with appetite, talking at the same time.

'I don't want the Maid to be a dreamer, you know. Joan's of the soil, a matter-of-fact female. A realist. A fine soldier and a born leader.'

'I know.'

'I know you *know*,' he said, slightly mimicking her voice's hoarseness and making her laugh. 'You may be completely aware that Joan is dogged and matter-of-fact, for all her saint's Voices. But you, Julie, are a bit of a dreamer. You'll have to give it up. Innocence, by all means. Fantasy, no.'

She had worked with him for weeks and she knew when to hold her tongue. It was only early in their relationship that she said or showed that she didn't get his points. Oh, those points Sir was always making!

Now she was confident with him except when they acted together, so she said nothing. She ate a small piece of chicken.

'The big parts need more than self-identification,' he went on. 'Melting yourself into Joan is good but it isn't enough. When you think about her, you must place her in the context of her own age; the girl who is a medieval oddity, not a creature of romance. She's a soldier and an excellent tactician.'

Julie quietly pushed her plate on to a side table and began to polish an apple, rubbing it along her old corduroy trousers. She took a bite which made a loud noise, a juicy crunch. Robert Waring looked surprised. He pushed his own plate to one side, walked over and put his hand under her chin.

'You know, *you're* a bit of a creature of romance,' he remarked, studying her. 'What goes on in that head, under that heartrending hair style I had the wit to choose for you? Are you frightened, Julie?'

She swallowed the pieces of apple, slightly choking.

'Not of you, Sir Robert.'

He sighed. 'I do wish you'd stop the Sir, Julie. It is very respectful and very right and proper and a drag. What about Robert? Come along now. Try it.'

'Robert,' she said experimentally. 'Robert. It's no good, it doesn't sound at all right. You're Sir. Everybody calls you Sir. Even Harriet.'

'But you are not Harry.'

She rather hoped he was going to leave her so that she could have another bite of apple in peace, but he remained standing by her, looking down at her intently. His beautiful face, his slanting eyes and cheek bones with Red Indian shadows, was pensive. His mouth was thin.

'Am I harsh on you?' he said at last. 'I try to be.'

'Oh. You succeed!'

'No sarcasm, Julie, that is my prerogative. Besides, it isn't in your personality. I think it probably never will be.'

For a moment, just one, she thought he was going to bend down and kiss her. She didn't know how she felt about this extraordinary thought . . . it was just there . . . Julie found she couldn't meet his eyes.

Then he moved away and she found she could breathe again.

'I'll walk with you to your front door when you have finished that *deafening* apple,' he said.

Julie had had no time yet to explore the little town of Condaford or the pleasant country neighbourhood, but she liked what she saw. Condaford was a market town, with a carved stone cross in the marketplace, and a church in a stately avenue of yew trees. The shops and hotels looked as if they were polished and poised for tourists, the lawns and gardens near the Festival centre were well tended and flowery. The place was prosperous. The Condaford Theatre, recently built as part of the Institute, was a mixture of concrete and pale wood, excellently designed and imaginative, with a shining glass front and engraved glass doors admired by visiting Americans. The Arts buildings included lecture halls, galleries, a library and a pleasant restaurant used by theatre-goers and other visitors.

The actors rehearsing *Joan* were looking forward to using the actual theatre stage for their rehearsals but at present the touring opera season was still in progress.

Chris, buying Julie an inevitable coffee in the Green Room, informed her that the opera wasn't playing to full houses. 'There are a lot of gaping seats like missing teeth,' he remarked with relish. '*We* are sold out for the first month.'

'Don't scare me, Chris.'

'You don't want to play *Joan* to a lot of missing teeth, stupid,' he said, laughing. He looked at her for a moment as she drank her coffee, cradling the mug with both hands. He added : 'I know how you feel, love. You want the play to pack. And yet you want to go on doing it in rehearsal and keeping your performance a sort of awful old secret!'

'Awful is right,' said Julie with a flip note in her voice.

But Chris had interpreted her thoughts with truth. She did, of course, want *Joan* to play to full houses, and she did, unreasonably, want to keep her performance secret from the outside world. When people other than pros actually saw her play Saint Joan, she would know if she'd succeeded or failed. And perhaps the saint's enigmatic personality would desert her.

The secret that Julie was busy creating with the other actors and Sir Robert was shared by one other person – Lisa Minton.

Miss Minton worked on what was called 'movement'. She had worked with Sir Robert for years. In appearance she reminded Julie of a wise, ageless animal. Her face was long, heavy and velvety, like a reindeer's or an elk's, her body was supple, whippy, bendable and moved with easy grace. Julie and four of the leading actors attended Miss Minton's classes daily. These were held in a small rehearsal room early every morning, and Lisa Minton arrived ten minutes beforehand for her own routine of brief, rigorous exercise.

Her classes took a formal pattern like a dance, and this was enhanced by the garment she wore, which could not be called a dress. It was made of fine, heavy grey jersey, cut to cling and hang. The robe touched the ground and was used in countless ways; she tucked it up when exercising, she folded it and rolled it, threw it sideways in an arc, knotted it, draped it. It was part of her teaching, part of its wearer.

As Julie came in this morning, Lisa Minton, the robe rolled above her knees, was seated in the Lotus position which only Buddhists, acrobats and dancers can achieve.

'Join me, Julie,' she said, without turning round to see who had come into the room. 'Sit beside me. That's right. Straight back. Back erect. Remember it is where your strength must always lie, in your back. It makes you strong. All your control, your power, comes from your back.'

Julie sat on the ground and Lisa Minton breathed deeply, rhythmically, expounding theories. Julie must place her voice *so*, hold her jaw *so*, speak *so*, breathe *so*. She must remember her back, lose her tenseness. Julie let herself be commanded, taught. Lisa Minton's lessons made her mind alert and clear, her body obedient. Lisa's voice was sonorous, it had a slight (never explained) accent.

'Now up. Move like this,' said Lisa, leaping up and taking a huge lunge forward. 'When you are fighting, you must move like lightning, when your enemy raises his sword, you must move thus, and thus . . .'

The tall figure fell into exquisite postures, the robe somehow indicated armour.

The four actors had arrived now and the lesson progressed.

When it was over, Lisa Minton was not even out of breath, though her pupils were sweating. She unknotted her robe, and rearranged her grey hair worn on top of her head in a small plait like a loaf.

Julie went across to thank her. Lisa regarded her.

'You must do a little course of exercises at night, I think,' she said. 'I will give you nine that must not be forgotten. They will take thirty-seven minutes.'

'Thank you, Miss Minton.'

'And remember your back. Straight, but giving a little.' Lisa Minton put a capable hand in the small of Julie's back and forced her to stand erect. Teacher and pupil stood close, Lisa muttering 'Straight, but relaxed.'

The door swung open and Daniel and Robert Waring came into the room.

'No, no, not like that. You've tensed yourself into knots!' exclaimed Lisa reproachfully. She patted Julie's back, murmured instructions and at the same time glanced over to where Julie was looking and noted Robert Waring and the young designer, apparently in argument.

'There, there,' said Lisa Minton soothingly. 'Sir Bobby must not disturb you. He enjoys a dispute.'

Julie was leaving the room with the other actors when Robert Waring beckoned.

'Julie! Come here!'

He was holding a design in his hand and frowning down at it.

'Have you seen your Rheims costume?' he enquired. 'I'm disappointed in it.'

'Sir Robert does not want Joan to be in white and gold,' Daniel said.

Both men looked at her.

Robert Waring had that bland look he sometimes wore at

rehearsals : it was a look that worried actors. There was a touch of malicious humour in it and his eyes, edged with long lashes, sparkled. But when Julie glanced briefly at Daniel, she saw that his face was composed and set. Daniel had once told her he liked people to show their feelings because he always showed his. Dealing with Sir was teaching him otherwise.

All the same, she had a distracted moment of thinking that Sir was hurting him, however coolly he was taking it. And another moment of remembering Daniel disliked her playing fairy godmother.

'I've seen the design already. It's sensational,' she said to Sir Robert.

'Maybe, maybe,' he answered, holding the drawing at arm's length beside Julie and narrowing his eyes. 'I don't deny it's a good piece of work and quite handsome in its way. The trouble is that it's romantic. Dammit, Monteith, it *is* romantic and it just won't do.'

Both young people looked at the star.

Julie thought : It's my turn to play it cool. It was *her* costume and *her* big scene in Rheims Cathedral . . . and hadn't Sir once told her costumes were vitally important to actors and helped them with a performance more than the actor himself knew? She said, 'The play says Joan is "splendidly arrayed". White and gold is splendid.'

'It isn't correct for the 1400s,' said Robert Waring, scratching his eyebrow delicately.

Daniel did not bother to reply. He knew that Sir knew the drawing was authentic.

Julie said, 'You told me only yesterday that, however discouraged she gets, it's still her glorious moment when she gets the King crowned and anointed, because she's done what her Voices told her to do. She wants to look wonderful just this once. Or perhaps she does it for the common people . . .'

'Little saint,' said Robert Waring, interrupting her but smiling as if the speech pleased him. 'All right, all right. You can have your splendid array if it makes you happy.'

He handed the design back to Daniel and patted Julie's shoulder. He left them and went across the room to Lisa Minton. But as he walked away he called over his shoulder, 'I still think it isn't 1400.'

When Julie looked at Daniel, he was white in the face. He walked out of the room.

The following days were getting uncomfortably near the

First Night, and meant more and more concentrated work. Julie scarcely saw Daniel again. He loomed . . . it was the word she used in her mind for his tall figure . . . in the distance, talking to actors. His serious face was lit sometimes with a smile. Julie had a stupid pang when she saw him smile at other people. When she went to the Wardrobe for her fittings, Daniel came too, and discussed each costume with her. He treated her as interestedly and disinterestedly as a doctor might do.

One evening, Daniel asked Julie if she could call at the laundry room when she was at Ravenfield some time. Julie's section of work at the rehearsal was over and she took a taxi back to Ravenfield. The sun had been shining heartlessly all day, and Julie found it dazzling to see bright day as she came out of the rehearsal room.

As she walked up Ravenfield drive, with tall flowers on either side, she thought about Daniel whom she had not seen for days. Now she came to think of it, she hadn't 'seen' Daniel as a friend and not a chill stranger since those far-off days at the Sheridan, before Robert Waring came like destiny into her life.

She turned into the courtyard and a voice called 'Hi!' It was Clover leaning out of an upstairs window.

'I've been looking out for you. Come on up.' Clover was shy; she always was with women, particularly leading actresses. Clover was at home with men; artistic ones and dotty ones, dedicated and temperamental and catty ones, the artists of the theatre. Julie, reserved and serious, was uncomfortable to be with sometimes. But when Julie came into the laundry room she was scarcely looking the 'leading actress'. She was tired and pale as Clover, and her practice clothes were dusty from spending half an hour during a rehearsal lying on the floor.

'Dan isn't here, he had to see Sir. He asked me to show something to you,' Clover said. 'Dan says actors sometimes like to see their costumes in private. You know, without the Wardrobe people fussing round. He says it can help to see a costume without being *nudged* into opinions . . .'

Clover went into another room, and came back with a costume over her arm.

'Joan. Act One,' she said, and held up a dark red dress. It was quite plain, with lacing at the simple round neck. The sleeves were long and comfortable, the waist was loose, the skirt full.

'It is exactly 1430, to the way the eyelets are sewn,' Clover said. 'And the fabric has been woven by hand. Shall we put it on?'

Julie peeled off her practice clothes and Clover slipped the dress over her head. It had no fastenings but the neck lacing; it was soft to the touch and comfortable. In a way, a timeless, antique way, it reminded Julie of the robe worn by Lisa Minton.

She stood in front of the wall mirror, and Clover, behind her, peered over her shoulder like a benevolent sprite.

'Do you like it?'

Julie moved and the dress swung as gently. It was so homely. So comfortable and homely. It was a country dress for a country girl whom Sir Robert had said was a creature of field and pasture.

'Very, very much,' she murmured to the little figure behind her shoulder.

Clover gave a satisfied sigh.

'Dan will be pleased. He asked me to show it to you and said how sorry he was not to be here. He's with Sir. A bit of trouble . . .'

When Clover helped her to take the dress off, Julie felt in some curious way that Joan herself vanished.

'Thank you for coming. And for being so sweet. Actors are often cross and fidgety, poor loves,' said Clover.

'You said Sir's being difficult. I wonder why?' said Julie. She said it to make conversation, she was still disturbed by the red dress which had made Joan more real than anything else until now.

'I don't know, Julie,' said Clover, hanging the dress carefully and covering it with a piece of white silk. 'Chris said the other day some of the Royalty London people told him Sir's marvellous with designers . . . giving them ideas and encouragement. One of the big names said Sir was an *inspiration* for designers. But he's been rather awful with Dan.'

She turned to Julie, almost as if she expected Julie to explain the trouble. 'He's so picky about the sets. Criticizes everything. I mean not just this or that but the lot.'

'I'm sorry Sir's been difficult,' said Julie tactfully. 'But you and Daniel must be used to temperament. Daniel has broad shoulders,' murmured Julie in her rôle of comforter.

Clover stared at the floor for a moment or two. 'He doesn't sleep, you know. My room is on the ground floor facing this flat, and once or twice I've woken and looked out, and do you know Dan always, always has a light on. When I ask him afterwards he says he works at night but I don't believe it. He doesn't sleep. He looks like a sheet sometimes.'

Julie listened painfully. She picked up her sling bag and the tattered copy of *Joan* which she carried about with her like a talisman.

'You're very fond of Daniel.'

'Everybody is,' said Clover with a little laugh. 'People can't resist him. Least of all *me*!'

When Julie had returned to the rehearsal rooms she sat on a bench watching Sir Robert rehearsing a scene with the Earl of Warwick. The rôle was played by Bryan Grant, a tall, impressive actor with a strong stage presence. She watched Bryan for a while, admiring his easy aristocratic manner, and listened to Warwick's speeches. But for once her mind wandered from the play. She thought of what Clover had said about Daniel; he was so close to her – a few walls away – and so wakeful through the night. He was a self-sufficient person, so much his own man, talented and – when she'd first known him – happy. Why couldn't Robert leave him alone? He'd chosen him to design *Joan*, so why must he pick on Daniel and worry him at this important time? She looked at Robert Waring, who was rehearsing Bryan in Warwick's scene with the representatives of the Church.

Robert, sitting beside Bryan on a stool, was clenching his fist and smiling. 'In this scene Warwick's cordial. He's always the soul of politeness – a real seigneur. He's courtly, always willing to make a dry joke or two. But *iron*. He is *it*!'

Julie thought that exactly described Robert himself. She wondered whether she could have a softening influence on Daniel's behalf over somebody who was *iron* and who was *it*.

She didn't notice that in her mind she'd begun to call Robert by his Christian name.

But the opportunity to say something kind or tactful about Daniel to Robert did not arise. No opportunity arose for anything but work. The opera company left Condaford. For the last few days before the Festival opening, the Company moved into the theatre for rehearsals.

The spirit of rehearsal changed when the actors were on the large, raked stage, with its apron thrust out into the audience, its rows of empty, expectant seats, its dark waiting auditorium. The pace quickened.

Daniel and Clover were working all day and much of the

night, spending their time at the laundry room or in the Wardrobe; people shuttled to and fro from Ravenfield, fittings were arranged hourly for the thirty-four actors in the cast of *Saint Joan*. Julie saw Daniel a number of times; he always came to see her costumes fitted and once, when she was dressed in her Rheims costume of white and gold, she thanked him for it and he smiled. The smile, which lit his handsome, serious face for a second, turned him into the young man who had made her so briefly, intensely happy. It was a shock to see that look again. But the look went and so did Daniel.

Robert Waring had many things on his mind, and daily meetings with the management, planning the next two productions to be added to *Saint Joan* in the repertory of the Festival. But he always had time for Julie; he was never tired of talking to her about the play and the 'little saint'. It was curious to think that this was the same man who kept Daniel awake by his criticism and sarcasm.

The other members of the Royalty company were soon used to seeing Robert Waring constantly with Julie. Riding in the car and walking across the lawns to the theatre, he always had the same companion, a short graceful girl with a soldier's haircut and big eyes in a thin pale face.

Harriet had been at the big house for some weeks now, the place ran as smoothly as Hampstead. When Robert and Julie returned from the theatre at night, there was always a meal waiting and Harriet there to greet them. Sometimes she left them alone. But she gave Julie a feeling of steady affection. In the high-strung world of the theatre, Harriet was the only one who stayed serene.

The night of the dress rehearsal arrived at last and Julie was intensely nervous. In her dressing-room she dressed slowly, taking a long time with the homespun red costume, her make-up, the thick long wig which she wore in the first act. She took a deep breath, remembering Lisa Minton's instructions; when she heard her call and went downstairs towards the stage her heart was thudding.

The play went well. Many of the performances were original, some of the actors brilliant. Sir's own performance that night, as the Inquisitor, was very dry and crisp; Julie had an idea he was keeping something back, and that next day, with an audience who loved him, he would alter and glow.

As for her own performance, she trailed back alone to her

new dressing-room almost in despair. She was wearing the white and gold costume in which Joan returns as a spirit in the last Act, long after her martyrdom. Glittering in white and gold, Julie went into the room, shut the door and leaned against it with her eyes closed.

She thought: I didn't do it; I can't do it. I'm not a good enough actress, I'm going to fail. The play is too great and I am much, much too small.

She stood for a long time with her eyes closed, wearing the warrior's costume and looking shrunken and small. At last, rousing herself, she slowly unbuckled her sword and noticed with surprise that she was shivering.

It was nearly one o'clock in the morning as she went down the long corridor of the theatre. Such a large handsome theatre, thought Julie, ready for such a big resounding failure for one little actress! She had changed now into her old practice clothes; with a thick black cardigan round her shoulders she was cold. It was only when she reached the stage door that she realized she'd forgotten to arrange with anyone returning to Ravenfield to give her a lift home.

Blinking in the wash of moonlight, she looked round the theatre gardens.

Robert's car was waiting, with the light switched on inside it, and Robert at the wheel.

'Julie!'

Suddenly, as if it had been yesterday, she remembered the first time he'd called her. The car had stood like a chariot of fate at the door of her shabby old digs. And Robert, fate itself, had come into her life with this huge awful chance which was going to ruin her career.

'Don't stand there in a trance, my dear girl.'

She climbed into the car and they drove back to Ravenfield.

Robert parked the car by the rose-beds and they went into the big house together. Neither had said a word.

There was no sign of Harriet or Sheba. A meal was laid in the terrace room but Robert poured Julie a glass of milk. She took it and went over and hunched herself into a chair.

He said nothing.

Suddenly she burst out, 'Robert, I can't do it! I don't know Joan . . . I don't understand her . . . I don't feel her! I don't know what Shaw is telling me and his Joan escapes me. She's so strong and sure but I shall never get to her, never! You shouldn't have chosen me, I am going to let you down, I shall

117

be an awful failure and you . . . you . . .'

She started to sob.

He sprang up as if he had been waiting for this, and came across and knelt beside her, putting his arms round her closely. She laid her head on his shoulder and cried as if her heart would break. She wept for the longed-for possession of the character who'd lived in her imagination all these weeks; she wept for a terrible doubt in her own talents. And because the man whose arms were round her had talent as huge as an enormous, breaking wave . . .

'There, there, cry away, that's right, do you good,' he murmured. 'Weep away. You'll feel better in a while.'

She was too tired and distraught at first to notice that she was in his arms, and when she was aware of it, it seemed sad and comforting that he . . . the one responsible for her grief and failure . . . should hold her close. She stopped sobbing, and he gave her a large clean handkerchief which smelled of the eau de cologne he used.

She mopped her face and somehow, before she moved out of his arms, he had let her go.

'Come and sit beside me. And stop crying, because you've done all that.'

They sat down on a sofa set against the glass wall facing the terrace. A vine grew there, covered with young tender leaves.

He put his arm along the top of the sofa, and she leaned against it, giving a shuddering sigh.

'Now listen to me,' he said. 'You are going to be good tomorrow, very good. Joan is almost with you, you need a very little step and you'll be there. Some of the time tonight you were absolutely right, quite perfect; at other times you were too subdued. Don't think about it *at all* until tomorrow night. Promise me. Sleep late in the morning and go to Lisa for your movement, and relax. All right? Better now?'

She gave another sobbing sigh.

'Julie,' he said, 'you have a very particular quality, I saw it in you the first time I set eyes on you. It's coming out, every day. All the Company are conscious of it, except you yourself. You have – you will have – something of a miraculous quality, a tragic feeling. It will come. You must believe me.'

She listened with painful attention. His voice was beautiful, it was like an instrument and it moved her. So did his sardonic face, with the irony gone and gentleness in its place.

'You look very weary,' he said, smiling in spite of himself, 'and very doleful. And very sweet. And very comic. Now, off to bed and sleep like the baby you are, before you break my heart!'

Julie did as he had told her. She went to her class with Lisa Minton and spent the rest of the day at home in her flat. She lay in the garden and tried to relax, but she was miserable and jumpy. The weather was dull and hot, the sky greyish, there was a distant growl of thunder. Julie hoped that perhaps Chris would call. But Chris was working. Julie forced herself to eat something for lunch but it seemed to choke her. She went back into the garden and lay, first on one elbow and then on the other.

The first night was due to start early – at half past six – so that critics would have time to telephone their notices over to London to catch the morning newspapers. Julie was beginning to think she must soon leave the garden and start for the theatre, when Harriet came through the french windows.

Harriet was looking unusually beautiful in a white silk dress and coat.

'I know I'm dressed far too early,' she said, 'but Sir's asked a whole lot of VIPs who are arriving in shoals and I've been given the job of looking after them. I came to say Sir's left you his car to drive you in. He's gone with Dan Monteith.'

'I thought Robert disliked Daniel Monteith,' Julie said listlessly.

Harriet thought she looked pathetic, sitting on the ground, staring at the grass. Harriet knew that look.

'Sir told me he thinks Monteith rather brilliant.'

'Oh Harry,' sighed Julie, 'that simply isn't true. I know everybody papers over Sir's faults and failings, but they don't have to do it with me. Robert doesn't like Daniel's work and I don't think he likes Daniel either.'

'That isn't what Sir told me, Julie,' Harriet said mildly. 'How can it be, considering Sir has asked Dan Monteith to design another Royalty production?'

Julie looked so surprised that Harriet laughed.

Harriet saw Julie into the car. Sir's impassive chauffeur was at the wheel, and Julie sat in the back, pressed in a corner like an orphan in a melodrama. Harriet bent forward and gave her a kiss.

'Good luck. I'll be out front, wishing it for you every minute. But I know, and Sir knows, that you're going to be all right.'

The car moved off, and Julie thought: I don't believe you, Harriet. I don't believe you, Robert. I suppose I must pretend I do.

Suddenly, after days of being 'dark', the Condaford theatre blazed. It was crowded, notices said 'House Full'. Suddenly the auditorium was filled to capacity with the buzz of twelve hundred voices falling to a hushed expectancy. Backstage were low, quick words as actors in costume stood in the corridor, or rustled by, cloaks swinging.

Julie was alone, wearing her homespun red dress and waiting for the intercom to begin relaying the voices at the start of the play. She sat looking at her own face, framed by the long, thick hair Joan wore when she was a country lass, before she became a soldier.

She thought: Where are you, Joan? She sat still, remembering Lisa Minton's instruction that her strength and poise and liberty of spirit came from her straight back. She thought about Joan . . . the ambassador of God . . . the eighteen-year-old soldier.

The door opened and Robert came into the room.

He took her by the hand and she stood up, and he said, 'Come along, little saint.' He walked with her in silence down towards the stage.

It was two in the morning and the play had been over for hours. All the audience's cars had driven away, the moon was shining on a sleeping town, the only lights now came from candles in branched stage candlesticks. These were flickering in the large and small rehearsal rooms where the first night party was milling with people and noisy with music.

The whole Royalty company was here tonight; not only the cast of *Joan* but many newly arrived actors who were being added to the numbers for *Faustus* and *Henry V*. Actors, wives and girl-friends were celebrating tonight's opening; so were the directors and Wardrobe people, so was Robert's tall daughter Candida, who had arrived with her husband for the performance, bringing loving messages from Tam. Tam was playing in London, so could not be present.

The rooms, set about with candles, were romantically dark and crowded. Bottles of wine stood on tables and chairs. Girls in long dresses danced barefoot; actors in jeans sat on ladders or the top of the piano or the rehearsal stage. There was an air of gaiety and abandon, exhaustion and merriment.

Julie was with Robert.

She was wearing a long white cotton dress sewn with Irish lace which she'd bought weeks ago and folded in a drawer and forgotten till now. In her elfin way she looked beautiful as well as tired. Her eyes shone, she looked tremulously happy.

For it had worked tonight. Robert was absolutely sure, Julie was almost sure, everybody else in the noisy candle-lit room was certain. It was strange to think it, but Julie had given what was called a 'star' performance this evening. The audience had felt something strong and tender for Julie, some peculiar feeling very like love, the feeling Julie had felt for them. The quality in her, more than any other, of being defenceless made them love her. She was cautious and brave but vulnerable.

Now, sitting watching the party by Robert's side, and now and again thanking somebody who came up to congratulate her, she was in a sort of dream.

'Do you want to dance, Julie?' Sir Robert said; they were sitting on the corner of the stage on two wooden seats. 'Or may I get you a glass of wine?'

'I couldn't dance a step. Or drink a thing. Thank you, Robert.'

'You'll disappear if I don't put a stop to it,' he said, touching her cheek. 'I won't have you turning into skin and bone.'

'Chris says you eventually turn all your actresses into what he calls skellingtons.'

'That,' said Robert mockingly, 'is because the poor things are inclined to fall in love with me.'

She laughed, conscious of his own consciousness of her. She thought: He *is* fond of me, and it gave her a sort of sad pleasure. She thought: I only feel safe when Robert is around.

She felt particularly attuned to Robert now, after the play. She had been right about his own performance – tonight it had been riveting. The Inquisitor remained the same character, but what had changed tonight had been an aura round Robert himself, something extraordinary created by the audience's feeling for him, and his power over, and need of, them. Julie had been awestruck as actors always were the first time they played at an opening with Robert Waring.

Now, as she and Robert talked and the party hummed round them, Lisa Minton came over. Lisa had shed her teaching robe but her dress tonight was very similar, a flowing garment of weighty black silk. She had pearls wound into her plaited hair, and Robert, quoting *Hamlet*, murmured 'Behold . . . the mobled Queen.'

Lisa asked him if he would come and talk to a new arrival, a young director who had driven down from London and whom Robert – and Lisa – were interested in.

'Will you forgive me for leaving you by yourself?' Robert said, taking Julie's hand and kissing her wrist. 'You won't be alone for two minutes, of course.'

When he had gone, Julie looked round the room and saw Chris and Clover dancing wildly together. Julie watched them with affection and gratitude – both had come rushing into her dressing-room at the end of the performance, their faces streaked with tears, to thank her and kiss her and gasp 'Oh, you were wonderful!' Julie felt the actress's humility and triumph at making people feel like that . . .

As she sat alone, a number of people came to talk to her and congratulate her. But they treated her in a different way from other actresses. Julie recognized the reserve was due to her relationship with Sir.

And where is Daniel? Julie thought. She had not seen him all evening. As if she'd conjured him, she caught sight of him on the other side of the room. He was leaning on the piano, his profile lit by the steadily burning candles. He turned and looked in her direction. Tired, blissful, too relaxed to think about the constraint between them, Julie beckoned to him.

He threaded his way through the dancers and she thought : How handsome you are. Dear Daniel . . . I nearly loved you . . .

As he came up she said in her hoarse little voice, 'I've been looking for you.'

'Have you, Julie?' He sat down on the stage at her feet. She looked down on to the top of his head; his thick glossy hair moved her. She wanted to touch it.

'I want to thank you, Daniel. For the designs. My designs. I love them and they do so much for me. They help me more than I can ever tell you. I think I understood the whole century because of your designs; it was my dress that really started to make Joan live for me.'

'It wasn't my work, Julie, though I'm proud to have helped you,' he said, looking up at her and speaking in a low voice. 'You were astonishing. So beautiful. You had us all in your hand. You must be very happy . . .'

Her eyes were full of tears.

'Julie. I want to say . . .'

His voice was low and she had to bend to catch the words; at that moment Robert came up to them. He was smiling and somehow, with a strong magic, he made both of them look at him.

'Dan, my boy,' he said cordially, 'I see you are playing courtier to the little saint. We can't have you stealing her away from me, you know. She has promised me what used to be called the Supper Dance. Come along, little Julie. You and I have a lot to celebrate!'

She never quite knew how it was, but Robert took her hand and whirled her away, and when she looked back Daniel had gone.

5

The TV caravans parked in Ravenfield's drive had electric cables looping out of them like stout snakes. The snakes threaded their way through the front door and across Harriet's elegantly-kept hall.

In the drawing-room, powerful lights were creating the glare of artificial sunlight in odd contrast to the dull day outside.

The TV interviewer, Howard Jackson, had been busy at what was called in the trade 'getting the best from the material'. This afternoon at Ravenfield his 'material' was Sir with Julie as second lead. Jackson had conversations with both of them, suggested his own questions to them and listened intently to their replies. Jackson, who'd known Sir for some time and actually called him 'Sir' as actors did, was a plump, prissy man with considerable charm. His methods with notables was to give them admiring and complete attention. Then, when actually on TV, he would pop in one or two uncomfortably probing questions. The viewers liked Jackson; some of the notables detested him.

Robert was not worried by Jackson's sharp reputation. Interviews did not worry Robert, who knew them to be useful and knew he could control them. He was looking, Julie thought, particularly stunning this afternoon. It often amused her to see how Robert dressed for the rôle of the day. It might be a denim suit (director), or old velvet (player), tweeds (financier), dark mohair (head of the Royalty). This afternoon Robert was in the rôle of star. He wore a navy silk suit of exquisite cut which showed off his muscular figure, a white shirt with a double pleat. He also wore, as part of the gear, a particularly aristocratic manner.

Jackson, clutching a mass of notes, was earnestly talking to the TV technicians. Robert and Julie sat with the relaxed patience of actors, drinking tea.

Howard Jackson hurried across the room to them looking worried.

'We're getting dazzle from the window behind you, Sir. And there's a bit of reflection on Miss Woods, too. I really am exceedingly sorry. Could we persuade you to move again?'

Robert raised his eyes heavenward. He and Julie had spent an hour being shifted round the room. They'd sat on chairs, stood by windows, posed by the fireplace, sat on more chairs. They remained equable, as actors always did. But there came a time . . .

'Have you no control at all over your damned machines?' sighed Robert, getting to his feet.

Jackson gave a sympathetic laugh and agreed that the cameras were a drag. Robert and Julie were settled on another settee, Jackson fussed round them, camera and lights were moved.

The interview started. Jackson asked Sir Robert the questions they had agreed; he also included a couple of sneaky ones that hadn't been mentioned. Robert was silky. Finally, the subject of Julie was introduced. Jackson, projecting charm to the camera, talked about Julie. 'This new young actress whose performance of *Saint Joan* brings us an astonishing newcomer . . . an important theatre discovery . . . original talent . . .' He asked Sir Robert how he'd found Julie.

Robert looked across at her with mock modesty. 'A great many people knew about Julie before I came along. My old friend Margery Wylie at the Sheridan, for instance, she cast Julie in *Much Ado* there. And then the Sheridan audience were very aware of Julie. I saw her. I had,' said Sir Robert, delicately scratching his nose, 'this idea of putting her into a taxing part . . . we talked . . .'

He beautifully shrugged, as if Julie's future had been fixed over a Coca Cola.

'Surely finding a new star isn't quite as simple as that?'

'Well . . .' said Robert, with a look from heavy-lidded eyes that implied he and Jackson shared exactly that magical skill. Finding stars over Coca Cola was an everyday occurrence for both of them. How could Jackson pursue the point?

Jackson then turned to Julie. When he began to talk to her she was conscious of the singular feeling of live TV. Everybody – Robert, Jackson, the crew behind the camera, the director watching beside them, was tensed and heightened by the medium. Yet it had a deceptive lack of drama.

'And how does it feel to become a star overnight?' asked Jackson, putting the words in ironic quotation marks.

Julie considered for a moment. 'I don't know. I can't really believe the star bit, though everybody's been marvellous about *Joan*. The thing is that I was almost certain, before it happened, I'd never get the part right. I was afraid of it. I thought I'd never discover how to get inside the character. Joan kept eluding me, she was always just out of my reach. But Sir Robert . . . he sort of inspired me, really. He taught me so much and gave me confidence and he *said* I'd do it. And I did,' she finished.

A pause.

'I think?' added Julie, tentatively.

Jackson and Robert genuinely laughed.

The interview ended with Jackson's formal 'Thank you, Sir Robert Waring and Julie Woods.'

The cameras stopped.

The tension snapped.

Jackson came over to thank them a second time, without his TV smile. 'It was great!' he said. 'Simply great!' He was delighted with the way the interview had gone, the worry vanished from his face, he looked ten years younger.

'I wonder . . . would you think it very tiresome to appear on my Sunday programme?' he said eagerly. 'You may have seen it sometimes; it's a revue of the week's big events. And as you're both very much part of the news this week . . .'

'Alas. Impossible,' drawled Sir Robert. '*Faustus* is already buzzing, I'm afraid. We're all slaves in the theatre, you know,' he added. 'No sooner have we pushed one safely out to sea, than we begin shoving another along. However, Julie is not in *Faustus*.' He glanced down at her. 'I'm sure she would like to be on your programme – Julie?'

She murmured something appropriate.

'I have an idea Julie may be one of those naturals with the camera,' Robert remarked.

'I agree,' said Jackson.

Jackson arranged for her to come to the TV Centre on Sunday afternoon when he recorded his programme. He thanked her effusively, giving her his powerful charm treatment. He shook Julie's hand, bowed goodbye to Sir. The cables were dragged out of the drawing-room, the cameras moved, the crew hustled together by their manager. In twenty minutes, everybody connected with the programme had driven away.

Harriet, Julie and Robert were left alone in a room which looked as if it had suffered a violent explosion.

Robert collapsed on the sofa.

'That wasn't bad. Jackson's a fly one. But we can manage *that*! You were nice, puss; he was looking at you like a boy through the tuck-shop window.'

'I thought *you* were lovely, you old Earl of Warwick,' she said, sitting beside him.

Harriet was amused at the confidence in the girl's voice. She offered Julie a plate of little home-made éclairs.

'Do have one. I made them for you, as a matter of fact. I've noticed your bones have started to stick out.'

Robert looked at his sister and raised his eyebrows.

'Don't give me that accusing glare, woman. I am not responsible for Julie's excesses. I merely told her to fine herself down. Eat away, puss. You have my permission to gorge yourself, for today anyway. But kindly don't burst out of your leather surcoat, it looks very nice as it is. Which reminds me, Harriet, I want to see Monteith about *Faustus*. Ask him and the little Clover girl round for a drink.'

'Of course. I'll telephone them now.'

Harriet left the room with her usual grace; her walk still had the ghost of the ballet about it.

There was a comfortable silence between them; Robert picked up some works and began to read, Julie sat with her hands in her lap and looked out at the summer rain. She thought about Daniel, who was coming to the big house for a drink. She would see him, and she wanted to. At the party last night he had been virtually taken away from her by Robert. She'd looked back at him, but Daniel had disappeared. Just before that, they'd talked together as friends for the first time for weeks and she'd thought they were going to say something – something worth talking about. She did want to talk naturally to Daniel again and stop feeling hurt over him. She wanted to thank him again for his designs which had been a kind of talisman helping her to find the spirit of *Joan* . . .

She looked out at the garden and thought : It *will* be all right between Daniel and me. Somehow today nothing could turn out badly!

She'd woken, and she'd read her notices. There had been a moment of disbelief and then a kind of wild joy. What Robert had told her had come true – she was a success. The first taste of fame had been astonishing : messages from her family, telephone calls, newspaper calls, TV offers, visits from friends, telegrams. And when she went to the theatre during the morning, bunches of flowers were waiting for her – left by loving strangers. Even now after all these hours Julie was a little punch-drunk with what had happened.

'It's a rum feeling. Enjoy it!' Robert had said, kissing her cheek.

Now, sitting beside him after the TV interview, she felt happy and relaxed; the alluring prospect of tonight's performance was ahead, the glow of the day still about her. Everything seemed to be coming her way. Of course she and Daniel would be friends.

Harriet came back, bringing the two Italian girls who had come down to Condaford with the Warings. The girls whisked round, removing traces of TV from tables, chairs and carpets.

Harriet said, 'Dan and Clover would love to come but they can't manage till eight, which is during Act One, Sir. That's all right, isn't it?'

'What a shame. I shan't see them,' said Julie.

Robert regarded her coolly. 'I'm not asking Monteith over for a *chat*, puss. It is for work. If you want to thank him for his designs, which I gather is in your mind, you have the rest of the season to do that. Anyway, it is I you should thank. I damn near re-designed the things, if you remember!'

She was disappointed that she didn't see Daniel, although she knew it was rather absurd of her. During the evening performance, working towards Joan's emotions, and then controlling the emotions she'd roused and making them work, Julie was lost in the mind of the Maid of Orleans. At the end of the play she heard again the roar of love and applause. The sound rang in her ears as she returned to her dressing-room.

Quite suddenly, as she sat down, Joan deserted her and she was Julie again. She felt dispirited, and the returning thought of Daniel made her eyes swim.

Still wearing her golden armour, she sat in front of the glass and looked at her face. She thought: I thought I'd never succeed and I *have*. I should be unbelievably grateful and happy. What am I doing, maundering over a man just because he's drifted away from me?

The dull weather changed, the bright summer returned. It was an exquisite morning when Sir saw Julie off from Ravenfield on her London trip. He instructed his chauffeur to 'take good care of Miss Woods.' The chauffeur saluted with a dedicated air of responsibility.

Robert, wearing denim and planning to work round the clock on *Faustus*, walked down the drive to see Julie off. He kissed her wrist.

'Be sure to go to bed early. I don't want you washed out when you return tomorrow. Kiss Tamara for me. I'll be up to see her performance at a matinée this week but I shall not tell her which one. God bless!'

He waved as the car went through the Ravenfield gates in the sunshine.

The journey to London was fast. Robert's chauffeur drove her to the TV Centre and arranged to collect her after the recording. Julie went into the building, as big and echoing as an airport, and asked for Howard Jackson.

'Miss Woods,' said the commissionaire. 'Mr Jackson has left instructions for you to be taken to Hospitality.'

As Julie followed a messenger down a number of corridors she was amused by the phrase. They passed what seemed like hundreds of closed doors until they finally arrived at one bearing the welcome word 'Hospitality'. She was ushered in.

'Oh Miss Woods!' exclaimed a big, plump girl, coming over. 'Jackson's in the studio. He'll be here very soon. I'm Shiona. May I get you a drink? Coffee?'

Shiona had freckles and a big smile. She pulled up a leather chair for Julie and settled her into it courteously. The room was rather dark, with numbers of chairs, tables, settees. Julie saw groups of people sitting in corners with coffee or drinks, muttering in low voices as if exchanging secrets.

Shiona looked so disappointed when Julie refused coffee or drinks that Julie felt bound to accept something. She might, otherwise, give the lie to the word on the door. When she said, 'A coffee would be delicious,' Shiona looked relieved and darted out of the room.

Julie picked up a magazine (about TV, of course) and was flipping through it when a voice said suddenly, 'Julie!'

It was Daniel.

She was so surprised that she blushed.

'What are you doing here – nobody told me –' she stammered. He laughed and sat beside her.

'I could say exactly the same. Nobody told me you'd be here either. The TV people telephoned me out of the blue last night about some designs I did for them, months ago. They shelved the programme and now they've revived it. I'm only here to give it a face-lift. A few hours and the job'll be done. What about you?'

She explained about the week's review of news. He listened and smiled. He had seen her on TV last night, he said, and enjoyed it. His manner was markedly different from his manner during these last weeks at Ravenfield, and Julie was pleased but almost astonished. What had changed Daniel back into this sweet, human person, laughing with her in this little dark room? They talked about *Joan*. But now it was as if the weeks gone by had been friendly and happy. Whatever had been in constraint between them was apparently gone.

He looked so handsome. Ah, thought Julie, whenever I see you, Daniel, I think that! His tall, graceful figure, expressive face, greenish eyes, and mouth that curled at the corners, were noticeably attractive. He was the sort of man women stare at. But during the last few weeks his expression when he was with her had been cold, and she had forgotten how fascinating he was when he laughed.

Shiona, returning with the coffee, looked disappointed at finding Julie with a companion. But when Julie introduced Daniel she cheered up and began to talk knowledgeably about TV sets and costumes.

Daniel and Julie listened politely. They hoped she would not stay. When she finally looked at an outsize wrist-watch, of the kind worn by deep-sea divers, she exclaimed, 'How dreadful, I have to leave you! Will you forgive me? I have to be On The Floor in two minutes' time.'

Julie and Daniel found it difficult to keep their faces straight.

'Howard will be with you *at once*,' promised Shiona, hurrying out.

They giggled when she had gone.

'I hope he isn't here at once,' Daniel said. 'There's something I want to ask you.'

'What is that?'

'Don't look worried. You do have the most expressive face. I was only going to say . . . if you would perhaps . . . if I could persuade you to have supper with me tonight?'

'I'd *love* to!'

She'd no idea why, sitting in 'Hospitality' among the dirty coffee cups, he was suddenly so kind and lovely and funny and familiar. It was a mystery she didn't want to solve. She was just glad and happy and they smiled at each other.

'We must fix it quickly before your producer comes and snatches you away,' he said. 'Where are you going to be this evening? And for how long?'

'Howard Jackson says the recording will be over by six. Probably before.'

'Mine will take longer, I'm afraid. Can I telephone you later?'

'I'm spending the night at the Warings' house in Hampstead,' she said. 'Ring me there. I'll be home and waiting.'

Daniel gave her an odd look. 'You're not going to be alone there, surely?'

She laughed. 'Harriet fixed for the Italian girls to come to London to keep me company. They wanted to see their boyfriends and jumped at the chance. Harriet said I'd hate being in that big place by myself. But the girls won't be back till all hours; I was going to watch telly and see myself on the box! Do ring. I'll be there from six for the rest of the evening.'

'Are you *sure*?'

'Of course,' she said simply. 'I'll wait for you.'

Ignoring the curious looks from a couple on the other side of the room, Daniel took her hand.

'You don't mind waiting for me? It's very sweet of you.'

'I shall want to.'

'I'll ring the moment I get away.'

At that moment Howard Jackson bustled in. Julie, signalling goodbye to Daniel and being answered with a wonderful smile, was hurried away, escorted down corridors and into lifts until, finally, they reached the studio.

The producer greeted her – literally – with open arms, crying 'Welcome!' It was the first time Julie had received star treatment; it made her rather shy. But she couldn't help enjoying it, as she enjoyed Robert's huge car, and the roar of applause after *Joan*, and the notices and . . . almost most of all . . . the flowers left for her by strangers at the stage door.

When the programme was finished, Howard Jackson took her back to the front entrance where Robert's car was waiting. She looked hopefully round for Daniel but there was no sign of him. Jackson and Shiona waved her goodbye and then vanished into their TV world of soundproofed rooms and clocks.

Robert's chauffeur, quietly driving the quiet car, said, 'Are we off to Miss Tam's now?' He liked Julie, and had privately told his wife he considered her 'a nice little friend for Sir's two nice girls.'

Julie said yes, and thank you. She lay back in the car, closing her eyes. She was full of the astonishing thought that she was going to spend this evening with Daniel. She had been right. Everything *was* going her way just now!

Tam and Julie hadn't met for weeks. Tam's play, written by her husband, had recently opened in London to chilly notices. David Bryden was a playwright the critics liked and they certainly loved Tamara, but they considered the new piece *Half in Half* was pretentious and that Tamara Waring had been wasted. Sir was not surprised by the notices, he knew the public disliked fantasy; Julie read them with dismay.

Now on her way to visit Tam she was in the odd situation of having succeeded, at present, more than Tam had done. She wished they had *both* had marvellous notices. But when she said this to Sir he had laughed.

'Success is like treacle. You can't have it for every meal. It'll do Tamara and David good to have a little salt instead.'

The car drew up at Tam's house, the studio-style windows were open and music was flooding out of them, filling the courtyard with the romantic sound of an operatic duet. A figure *should* have been leaning from the wooden balcony, singing of love. In actual fact Tam came pelting down the wooden staircase like a schoolboy.

'The girl herself, after weeks and weeks!' cried Tam, giving Julie a rib-cracking hug. 'Come on up to the flat and have a drink. Is Dixon staying for dinner?' she added, peering at the chauffeur who promptly said that it was kind of her but he had a date. 'Snooker!' said Tam, laughing. 'Come on, Julie. We must make the most of every minute!'

The girls went up the stairs to the room where the enticing music sang.

Tam chattered. She exclaimed over the fact that she had not been able to see *Joan*, at the 'dire' behaviour of her father who'd refused to let her speak to Julie on the telephone during rehearsals, and at Harriet's faithful relay of news.

Julie, listening, remembered exactly how it had been when they'd shared a dressing-room. Tam was so talkative, impulsive, generous, bossy, cheerful. And then occasionally so sunk in gloom! Today she was at her most glowing, in an embroidered peasant dress sewn with orange, yellow and marigold colours. Her hair hung in tawny loops on either side of a face covered in summer freckles.

'Dave's seeing a man who is translating the new play into Swedish. All Dave's plays go into Swedish, never into French. Must mean something! Wasn't it maddening I couldn't come down to your first night?' Tam sighed.

'But you had one, too, Tam. We haven't been to see *Half in Half*. How's it going?'

'Let's not mention it. Dave.was so cast down about the notices, but then he re-read them and suddenly shouted "Hell. They may be right!" Well, Julie, as I'm the actress still playing in the piece I found *that* unnerving, to put it mildly. Anyway, the dear boy has started writing something new which, of course, he hasn't told me about. David's a secret writer, he vanishes when he's working. And that leaves me playing *Half* every night on my own. I still love the play and I think the audience is building – a bit, anyway. But *Joan*'s a big thumping success, so why are we talking about me? Tell everything. Did Dad give you a worse time than he gave Candy, who was practically dead with nerves? Or me when I made the *Tempest* picture with him. I had a rough passage, I recall.'

They talked shop. The most delightful, alluring, impossible-to-stop conversation in the world, the talk theatre people never finish, a river that carries them all on its steady, never-ending stream.

Julie told Tam about the Condaford company, about Harriet, Chris, *Faustus*, *Joan*; Tam's eyes were intently fixed on Julie, her face changed as the tale changed.

'And what about Daniel? The notices said the designs were great.'

'They are. Daniel is so clever, isn't he, Tam? And he's done your production *and* ours.'

Julie's manner of speaking about Daniel was natural, happy even, and Tam, who had been aware in the past that something had separated Daniel and Julie, felt encouraged. Apparently it was all right now.

While the two girls talked, Julie glanced at the clock on the wall. It was an old ship's clock, in a circle of brass, and the thin hands showed that she had enough time to enjoy her visit with Tam and still get back to Hampstead before Daniel was due to telephone her.

Tam poured them a glass of sherry.

She said casually : 'By the way, I have a surprise for you.'

Tam's expression just then was the image of her father's. She wore the same confident glee, the air of a person who likes games and intends to win them.

'What are you up to, Tam?'

'*I'm* not up to anything !'

'I know that Waring face.'

Tam laughed. 'Well, let's say somebody else is up to something,' she said. 'Somebody Dad calls the old gnome of Wall Street.'

'Renfred?' said Julie, intrigued. Now and again Robert had talked about Renfred to Julie, always rather irritably. Renfred played an important part in Robert's life : the motion picture part. He usually seemed to be in America on the day (or hour) that Robert wanted him.

'Renfred wants to see us. He says he has something to talk to us about. He wants us *both*,' said Tam.

She paused, head on one side. 'He wouldn't say what it is about, though I wheedled away like anything. He just repeated he'd like us to have a glass of champagne with him. Of course I said super.'

'When are we going?'

'What's wrong with now?' Tam sprang to her feet like a dancer, in a single movement.

'Isn't it *interesting*? He rang again this afternoon to check if we were coming, and I was bursting to ask outright what he wanted, but he wouldn't have said. Why do you suppose he wants us? Why both of us?'

Julie did not answer at once; she was too embarrassed. She knew perfectly well, as Tam did, that Renfred's casual-seeming invitation was to do with work. She and Tam weren't being asked round socially but as actresses. She'd seen those little invitations before. Robert played it the same way – he'd done it with her ! And how was she going to get out of this one ?

'We ought to get going,' Tam said. 'Do you mind if we go

right away? Renfred said he had to go out later so he wants to see us early.'

There was still time – enough time – for Julie to accept and she did so with relief. But instinct told her not to mention when she had to be back at Robert's house, or that she was going to see Daniel.

'Where are we going to meet him?' she asked.

Tam laughed. 'We're going to his flat. You do keep your cool, Julie. *I'm* not cool. Suppose he offers us something amazing! Think of Dad's face.'

Tam was in high spirits as they drove through dusty London. The streets were crowded, the people had a holiday air. Tam was a nippy driver and her white Mini wove in and out of the traffic, finally drawing up in a side street off the Strand.

'This is Renfred's hideout. He really prefers being in suit-cases. Dad says Renfred's spiritual home is the Paris Ritz.'

The building was solid, old-fashioned, cool, quiet. The girls climbed a wide staircase.

'Most of the guys living here are barristers,' remarked Tam. 'When I come here with Dad we always meet a couple on the stairs. Dad said with those good profiles and ringing voices he wouldn't mind hiring them to carry spears.'

They stopped outside a door with a brass knocker shaped like a dolphin. Tam grasped the dolphin's tail and gave a loud rat-tat-tat.

'He'll know it's me. Renfred's friends are all quiet; rich people are.'

Renfred de Buisson opened the door. He looked his smooth, rosy-faced, white-haired, imperturbable self, and he smiled a welcome. He kissed Tam and pressed Julie's hand.

'Julie. I was in the States but I must have been mad not to cancel the trip and see your *Joan*,' he said. 'How kind of you both to visit me. Come in.'

The flat, like the block, was spacious and old-fashioned. He led the way into a big comfortable room, where a littered desk showed he had been at work. He welcomed the girls with a warmth specially his own, managing to talk to both of them about their work, making dry jokes. The girls reacted in their separate ways – Tam, who'd known him since she was six, with laughing replies, and Julie quietly, getting Renfred's points as quickly as she did Robert's.

Renfred looked interestedly at Julie. She was wearing a Greek-styled dress of olive green and cream bands and

squares. Her olive suède shoes had thongs crossed around her
ankles. The clothes were original and under-stated, just as
Tam's were exciting and eye-catching. Renfred, who liked
flowers, thought that the two girls resembled a rose and a
marigold in the same vase.

He poured them some champagne and said, 'You are both
looking at me somewhat expectantly.'

'We were both looking at you with our eyes popping out
of our heads,' said Tam, sounding so like her father that
Renfred burst out laughing.

'I usually prefer a little time . . . or room to manoeuvre,'
he said. 'However, I see that I shall be forced to get to the
point right away . . .'

'Please!'

'I wondered if you might be interested in appearing in my
picture.'

There was a speaking silence.

'In the Spanish epic?' exclaimed Tam. 'The tenth-century
one? Dad's one?'

'Precisely so.'

'But who are we playing? Who am I playing?' said Tam,
her affection for Julie and her actress's instinct running neck
and neck.

'I thought the rôle of the Aragon princess. She is Sir's
daughter in the picture,' Renfred said. 'The princess who is
abducted. It's a fascinating part . . . you'll see when you read
the script. It would mean rather a lot of work on location,
I'm afraid. And Julie, the rôle we had in mind for you is the
Princess's slave. She goes on a long journey . . . a kind of
Odyssey . . . and finally rescues her mistress.'

'I remember.' said Tam suddenly. 'Dad read the story
to me. Julie is the lead. *I'm* the comedian.'

'You know quite well that is an over-simplification,' said
Renfred coolly.

Tam laughed and said, 'Well, perhaps.'

He gave both the girls a copy of the script and said, 'I
realize I should have talked to you separately. It is not the
way to do things – to invite you to see me together. But you
are friends and will . . . suppose you accept . . . have a considerable amount of scenes together. I thought you'd like to
talk about the picture to me first and then perhaps discuss it
with one another. I realize you can't give me an answer yet.
But could we talk for a little?'

They began to discuss the film. Renfred described the

powerful story and his idea for making it a fable, using the word 'epic' in its true sense. He talked of the location, of the other actors, of timing, direction. Julie was as fascinated as Tam, and it was only after a length of time and a lot of talk that she glanced at her watch.

'I must go!' she exclaimed abruptly.

Renfred looked up. 'I've kept you too long. I'm so sorry, Julie. Our meeting was racing along and I forgot the time. Have you an appointment? Can I get you a taxi?'

'Could I telephone somebody first?' Julie said hurriedly. She was suddenly worried and ill at ease. It was an hour after the time she had told Daniel she would be home. She sprang to her feet.

Tam, with the delicacy she sometimes used with Julie, did not ask questions, and Renfred took Julie into his bedroom where there was a telephone.

When she was alone she rang the Hampstead number. She hoped the Italian girl Mia might be there and could take a message for Daniel. But the number rang and rang in the empty house. Julie visualized the stately room, with the silent roses outside in the garden and the bell shrilling within. Giving up at last, she rang the TV Centre. When she got through to the programme Daniel had been working on, a pleasant voice said that he'd been gone 'some time'.

She went back to the sitting-room. Renfred and Tam had resumed their conversation about the film and were amusing each other. They turned as she came in, the laughter fading in their faces as they saw her expression.

'I can't get a reply,' she said. 'If you could get me a taxi, Renfred, I would be grateful.'

She said goodbye, and promised to telephone in the morning to make a further appointment. She took the script of the film, and Tam kissed her and said 'Longing to talk!' Renfred accompanied her downstairs to the car and watched her drive away.

The moment the car had moved off, Julie leaned anxiously forward, wishing and wishing that the traffic could melt and she could be in Hampstead *now*!

But the journey was long. The traffic was thick. It was a long time before she paid the driver and ran into Robert's house, switching on lights to dispel the twilight.

The big place was in a hush of loneliness. She went into Robert's study and sat down at the desk, looking at the telephone. She didn't even open the film script she had in her hand.

She sat by the telephone for two hours . . .

Time dragged as if in the grip of disaster or grief. She rang his studio a number of times – no reply. It seemed to Julie the whole world was mute while she waited for Daniel's call which never came. In the end, utterly miserable, she trailed up to bed . . . but not to sleep.

In the morning, worn out and dark-eyed, she was awake when Mia brought her breakfast in. The moment Mia had left her, Julie rang Daniel's studio. To her infinite relief, a low voice said 'Yes?'

'Daniel! At last! It's Julie.'

'Where were you?'

It would have been an angry voice if it had not been a cold one.

'I was late. I got held up. I got back at – '

'I rang you every quarter of an hour from six until nearly nine o'clock. I thought you'd been in an accident.'

'I was stuck in a traffic jam. I'm terribly sorry, Daniel, it was *maddening*. But I had to see Renfred unexpectedly about work and . . .'

'Don't make excuses like a stupid child. I am not interested. We called it off once before, remember? That was right. The first time was right. Forget it, Julie.'

He slammed down the receiver.

The car called for Julie after lunch and she drove back to Condaford on a brilliantly sunny afternoon. The chauffeur was silent and Julie didn't say a word. She looked out at the long white roads, and now and again at birds, flying high, in couples, their wings warmed by the sun. She didn't blame Daniel for being angry and for telling her he did not want her. She thought: It's ironic. For both times with Daniel have been spoiled because of something to do with my job. My being an actress. Being *me*. She looked, dry-eyed, out of the car window. The window was open, and the smell of the country blew in, of growing things and hay and flowers. In a way, Julie thought, she was imprisoned in the rich car which was driving towards a further imprisonment. The work that swallowed her life, demanded all her imagination, all herself. And now it was taking her away from the man she might perhaps have loved. She drove all the way to Condaford with the thought that she was a prisoner. And that the person who'd built her prison was herself.

The car drew up at the stage door, where a few visitors were lingering. Julie was stared at as she jumped out of the car, and one or two of the more dashing fans asked for her autograph. She smiled and scribbled, thanked them for their good wishes, and ran through the stage door.

The stage doorkeeper leaned from his cubbyhole and called out to her, 'Miss Woods. Bin waiting for you. Miss Waring said to ring right away. I'll get you the number. Lady said it was urgent.'

Now what? thought Julie, as the stage door keeper painstakingly dialled the number.

He handed her the telephone.

'Harriet? Me. I just got back.'

'Julie! Thank God. Can you come right away? It's Sir.'

'What do you mean?' gasped Julie. She felt quite faint.

'He's had an accident. He wants to see you. Hurry.'

She didn't remember the journey back to Ravenfield. She put down the telephone and rushed out to the car, which drove her back to the house at once. The front door was open and Harriet was waiting. Harriet, in a grey dress, and with a grey face, came over and grasped her hands.

'Thank heaven you're back, darling. He's upstairs in his room. It's his arm. It happened at rehearsal today; they think it's broken. Go up right away. He's been asking for you ever since it happened.'

Julie didn't know whether to be relieved or frightened as she ran up the staircase and down the corridor to Robert's bedroom overlooking the garden. She knocked on the door and an unmistakable voice, quieter than usual, said, 'Come'.

Robert was lying in bed, his arm and shoulder heavily bandaged, his beautiful face the colour of the sheets. His hair fell across his forehead, and this look of exhaustion and disarray was so strange that for a moment she did not see him as the star at all – but as a wounded stranger.

She ran across the room.

'Julie,' he said, with a slight smile and a grimace. 'Where have you been, child?'

'I got back a moment ago. What happened?'

He shifted, grimacing again, and said, 'Didn't Harry tell you?'

'No.'

She pulled up a chair and leaned close to him, and he

138

grasped her hand with his own unbandaged one.

'I was doing the *Faustus* leap. It's from the high stage and I've done it a hundred times before. It's simple if you know how. It was my own fault today; I fell wrong. Right down on to my shoulder.'

'Robert!'

He regarded her for a moment ruefully as she stared at him.

'Dear girl, don't look so woebegone. It's not all that bad, you know. But I may have broken it and that won't be funny. They're doing the X-ray later. In the meantime, all I have to do is to keep still.'

He said this with faint irony. Julie felt an extraordinary out-of-proportion grief. It was like seeing an eagle with a damaged wing. The creature was meant to fly at enormous heights above the clouds, to sweep in liberty, power, solitude. What was her eagle doing, lying there so broken?

'What can I do for you, Robert?'

'Stop trembling to begin with,' he said, smiling, but with an effort. 'I want to talk to you about *Joan*. William Hewitt is understudying for the Inquisitor, as you know, but we've had far too few understudy rehearsals. I don't want you thrown when you do your scenes with him. Listen, now . . .'

She held his hand and listened intently while he talked about her rôle, the play, the man who was replacing him tonight. Even now, Robert was thinking about *her*. His complex, crowded, demanding, busy life was in an appalling dilemma; he was in pain. He thought of her.

'Yes. Yes, I've got it. I'll remember everything. I know it'll be all right. But, Robert, *please* don't think about me. Can't you sleep? I am sure it is hurting you.'

'A bit. Not too bad.'

'I don't believe you.'

'I feel better now you are back,' he said. 'Puss . . . I thought – I don't know what I thought. Come and see me after the performance.'

'You may be asleep then.'

'I will not be, Julie.'

He looked at her fixedly for a moment and then said, 'Go now.'

'Yes, Robert.'

'Kiss me,' he said. She bent and kissed him, and when she opened her eyes he was still looking at her, with an expression she didn't understand.

'I'll see you after the performance, little saint.'

The performance that night was packed, as every Condaford performance of *Saint Joan* was packed. The audience was patently disappointed by Sir Robert not playing, and the auditorium was littered with the sad little slips which said 'The management greatly regrets . . .' But, as was so often the way at times when a great star is missing, the audience was particularly kind. They gave the play, and Robert's understudy, a long, affectionate reception at the end.

Backstage, the company was subdued and quiet. People whispered. Faces were anxious. The news had already leaked out, it was on TV, and journalists had started to crowd into the theatre. Chris came into Julie's dressing-room as she hastily finished dressing. He was subdued too.

'I have a message from Harriet. She says you must leave by the little door into the garden. The press are buzzing too much everywhere else. The car's waiting there. Cheer up, love. He's going to be all right. You know he's as strong as an ox!' added Chris comfortingly.

Julie, wearing a dark coat, slipped from the side door and was driven back to Ravenfield.

All the actors and other occupants of Ravenfield were home, there was a mass of cars parked by the rose-beds. Only Daniel's car was missing, and Julie thought : He's still in London. Daniel's unkind voice this morning seemed a million years away, like a bad dream. What was real was the big house, shining with lights in every window.

Harriet came to the door. She had changed out of her old grey dress into a rose-coloured one and looked better. She and Julie kissed.

'The arm was X-rayed and it isn't broken,' Harriet said. 'Which is a miracle as he fell on it from about fifteen feet up from the high stage. It's very badly bruised and hellishly painful. He's got to keep it immobile for the time being, and the doctor says he has to stay in bed for the next few days. He looks *awful* but he keeps on working. He had six people in this afternoon, and he was on the telephone for an hour. It's ridiculous. However, I put a sleeping pill into his coffee. That's knocked him out for the moment.'

'Are you worried about him?' Julie said. Like Harriet, her face was white. She was wearing the Greek dress Renfred had admired, but the soft, pretty look about her was gone. She looked drained. Harriet thought what a tender person Julie was, with her gentle manner and round face, and big, generous mouth.

'Go up and sit with him, Julie,' she said. 'He told me you were coming. He'll be disappointed when he wakes if you are not there.'

The words, the tone, didn't sound as if Harriet were talking about her brother. They were touching and when was Robert ever that, save in his art? They were pathetic and when was Robert ever that, save on a stage?

Moonlight shone through the corridor window; Julie went quietly into Robert's room, which was dimmed; there was only one shaded light on the desk by the open window. Robert was asleep.

He lay against a heap of pillows, the bandages wound round his shoulder and arm. His face was ashen, and the dark hair, streaked with grey, fell across his forehead in an unfamiliar curl. She stood staring down at him. He looked like a dying poet. Like a beautiful dying poet, stricken to death by love and sorrow.

She pulled up a chair and sat beside him.

The night at Ravenfield was quiet. There was no traffic. An owl hooted as it flew over the house, and a clock ticked hurriedly from the other side of the room. Robert slept, his long lashes closed over his clever eyes, his face reposed and pale.

She sat watching him and thinking about him; about his magnetic, masculine force, his intensity of acting, his nobility, his character of paradox. She thought about losing Daniel. She thought about the long, quiet night.

At last, with scarcely a flutter of eyelashes, he drowsily opened his eyes.

'How long have you been sitting here?'

'Not long.'

'Liar.'

He looked at her for a while and she had a sweep of sad, sad longing. Oh Robert! Don't look like that! Don't look as if you *suffer*. You are the great actor, the strong one, the leader, the genius. You mesmerize us, enslave us. Don't look like that, with those beautiful, wounded eyes!

'How are you, darling?' she said and he smiled.

'That is the first time you have called me that.'

'Oh. I didn't notice.'

141

'It's a worn-out old word, isn't it?'

'It isn't worn out when it is meant,' she said, and stumbled over a sob.

She leaned forward to grasp his hand and he said slowly, 'It's curious how I wanted you here after it happened. I was worried about you. I thought – I don't know. That something had happened to you and that you were in trouble. I had an absurd idea that you would not come back to play *Joan* and that if you did not . . . I don't know what I thought.'

He stopped speaking and they were silent for a while. She leaned close, holding his hand. The room was dim, the night was quiet. The owl hooted again in a melancholy, drawn-out sound which floated over the rooftops.

'Julie,' he said at last.

He was looking at her with intensity and she answered in a low voice, 'Yes, Robert.'

'I want to say something to you. Can you guess what it is?'

'No. What do you want to tell me?' she said, leaning forward and holding his hand tightly in her own.

She truly did not know.

'I think perhaps it is to tell you that I love you,' he said. And smiled.

6

There was a moment of complete stillness. It seemed to Julie that she and the night both held their breath.

He gazed at her in the dim light and said thoughtfully, 'It's a wonder to me that I could fall in love. But I find that I have. You haunt me. I catch myself thinking about you so much, too much, far, far too much. Your face comes into my mind when I am alone, when I am working, when I am asleep. Such a funny face . . . with those big eyes and that solemn expression of yours. You are looking very solemn now, Julie. As if you were in church. Sweet, funny, brave, steady, *real* girl!'

She was trembling. She did not know what to say – what to think; she put down her head and hid her face against his hand.

'I would like you to marry me, you know,' said the hushed, moving, practised voice above her, the voice that knew exactly how to break hearts and command tears all over the world.

These extraordinary words made Julie look up. For a moment she could not believe them.

'Marry you!'

The pale man, lying against the pillows, smiled again.

'Of course. Marry me. Does that sound strange?'

'Yes – no – I don't know – '

'Ah Julie, don't look like that. You look frightened. You are never frightened of me, remember? Why should you look alarmed because I ask you to be my wife?'

'I – I never thought . . . I didn't know . . .' There seemed no answer to his question, his declaration of love, his exhausted face like that of a dying poet, his beauty and pain, but tears. And one could not just lie with one's head on Robert's arm and cry like a stupid child!

'I didn't ever guess you loved me and it is beautiful to hear it and I don't know what to say,' she said, kissing his hand. 'But won't you please get better first?'

'Perhaps that would be wise.'

'You are laughing at me.'

'Of course.'

There was a pause.

She stood up and looked down at him. She bent and kissed him. They kissed for a little time and he put up his hand and laid it against her cheek. When she opened her eyes, his were still closed. He looked ashen, and she had a pang as sharp as a knife in her heart.

'Good night, darling Robert.'

'Good night, little saint.'

'Can we talk tomorrow?'

'Please.'

When she had left the room, and walked down the dark staircase, she suddenly thought how strange it was to hear Robert say that.

She passed quietly as a ghost across the stableyard. Daniel's flat was unlit. She opened her own front door and wandered into the room without putting on the light. The flat was warm from the sun of the day gone by and smelled of dying honeysuckle. The curtains were back and the faint light of a starry night fell in a radiance on to the floor.

She sat down on her bed, in the room with its smell of fading flowers, and she thought: What just happened can't be true.

A few moments ago Robert had held her hand and asked her to marry him, telling her that he loved her. The idea was so vast that Julie sat for a long time contemplating it. A few weeks ago she'd been the mouse of the Rep, hoping she wouldn't have to be patronized by an actress's world-famous father. And now . . . The change almost appalled her.

How did it feel to be loved by Robert? It gave her a kind of awe, a feeling of responsibility, the curious sensation that she did not deserve his love, that its magnetic force was too great for her. She thought of him in a hundred different moods. He was the director, clever, powerfully intelligent, penetrating, a conductor who could bring music from every instrument in the orchestra. He was the father, affectionate and teasing with his daughters, treating them like an aristocratic parent in a Victorian novel and being teased in return. He was the head of a huge theatre ensemble, involved in plays and their players, foreign tours, money, dealing with infinitely temperamental people who made up the world where he was king. Above all, he was the actor who had a generation in love with him – the magnetic actor, with humour, tragedy, force, heart-tearing talent, the actor you *had* to watch, the genius who gripped your heart.

'How can one marry a genius?' she said aloud, and as she spoke the words alone in the starry room they sounded as if they came from a play.

Emotion had worn her out and she slept late into the morning. There was no call for rehearsal, and when she woke it was broad daylight and she remembered immediately that Robert was ill. She pulled on her practice clothes, splashed her face with cold water and ran out into the yard. She rushed up to the front door of the big house. Harriet was in the hall, talking to Mia.

'How is he?' Julie said, standing in the doorway.

Harriet came across to her. Her unhurried walk and her fresh white silk overall made the day more cheerful, Julie thought.

'Better. More comfortable. He had a good night, and the doctor is with him now. He wants you to lunch with him.'

'I'd love to.'

'I'll tell him you're coming,' Harriet said. She saw that Julie had only just woken up, and indicated in the Waring way that often used no words, that Julie needn't feel bound to stay but could go back to her flat and have breakfast with a peaceful mind.

Julie thanked her and went back to a bath and coffee. She put on jeans and an old white T shirt and sat in the garden for a while. But she couldn't settle. She was fidgety and uneasy. In broad daylight, sunlight, with birds singing and the sound of voices from other flats in Ravenfield, last night seemed more extraordinary than ever. I must tell somebody, she thought; but the only person she really wanted to tell was Daniel.

She felt lonely and she wanted to see Daniel so much. He had been angry with her, but everything was different now, surely he'd help her when she was so worried. She needed him.

The door of the laundry flat was ajar, and she noticed that Daniel's car was parked beside the rose-beds. She wondered if Clover was with him and what she would say in front of Clover . . . but before she'd decided what she was going to do, she was in the laundry room and had found Daniel alone.

He was sitting at a table, working at a detailed design of a man in a black and gold costume, wearing a heavy chain and a mantle edged with sable. Daniel, intently working, did not hear Julie come into the room. She gave a little cough.

When he saw her he did not stand up, but sat, paint-brush in hand, gazing at her.

'Can I talk to you?'

He frowned irritably. 'I really think it would be better not.'

His tone was back to the old Daniel, the cold Daniel, but Julie had been expecting it.

'It's not about us – I mean, it isn't about the other night. I know you're still angry with me though I did apologize.'

'Nothing is easier than apologies. Leave it, please.'

At any other time the insultingly brusque manner would have sent her rushing from the room, but she persevered. She said, 'It isn't about you and me. Truly. It's just about me. I need your help.'

'How could you possibly need that?'

'Oh, don't sound so jeering. Just listen for a little while. I won't keep you long.'

He did not reply and she sat down on a chair.

'Did you know Sir has broken his arm?'

'The whole of the United Kingdom knows that. It was on TV and in this morning's papers and anyway it's not broken.'

He had put his paint-brush into the gold paint and had begun to work.

"I wish you'd stop being so angry and rude,' she said, sighing. 'I told you I wanted your help. I would be grateful for it. I can't tell you if you keep biting my head off. It's difficult to talk to you. You're so spiky it is quite painful. I wanted to say that I went to see Sir last night when I got back after *Joan* and he did look awful, poor darling. He must have been in great pain. He was asleep but he looked sort of haggard and worn out. And then he woke up and I talked to him for a bit and then – and then he asked me to marry him.'

Daniel stopped painting.

'You don't look very surprised,' Julie said, swallowing.

'I am not in the least surprised,' he remarked coldly. 'And if you are frank, Julie, neither are you.'

'I don't know what you mean.'

His manner had finally upset her after her determination not to be hurt. Her eyes filled with tears which she shook angrily away.

'I mean that Sir Robert and you have been the talk of the place since you arrived. You've never been out of his pocket. It was patently obvious how he felt from the start. So spare me the girlish bit about how staggered you are that he's asked you to be his wife.'

'But I *was*,' she said stubbornly. 'I was astonished. I didn't know he felt like that. I don't care if you believe that or not.'

'Oh, for God's sake!'

He picked up his paint-brush and then threw it down. His face looked pinched. There were shadows round his mouth.

'What did you come over to tell me this for? Am I expected to congratulate you? Very well. I do. I congratulate you.'

'I haven't said I'll marry him and I don't know why you're so horrible, Daniel. How *can* you!'

'Now, Julie, don't be ridiculous,' he said, his voice kinder, embarrassed even, as he looked at the small sobbing figure. 'I'm sorry I sounded rude. You and Sir irritate me. Other people's love affairs are always a great old bore. Please don't be upset. I'm sorry I was rude,' he repeated.

But he didn't go near her and his expression was blank. In a way his apology was worse than his being harsh. She knew the meeting was over and had come to nothing. Oh, what had she hoped might come of it?

She stood up, wiping away the tears with the back of her hand like a schoolboy. She didn't speak to him again but went out of the studio, and down the stairs, and out into the sunshine.

Clover enjoyed research almost as much as actually working on designs with Daniel; she had spent an interesting and fruitful week in London. She had been commissioned by Daniel to get as much material as possible for *Faustus*. Her research had led her through books of German myth and magic, books of strangely assorted rituals with woodcut illustrations of ceremonies and incantations, facts about witches and warlocks. She had books on *Faustus*'s city, castles and churches, vestments and costumes.

She was feeling tired but cheerful as she stepped off the train at Condaford, dragging with her a huge suitcase weighed down with books.

She took a taxi to Ravenfield and spent the journey there leaning out of the car window to see if she could catch sight of any of the Festival actors.

She had been away over a week and had missed the excitement of Sir's injury. Seeing the news on TV and Sir's photograph in the newspapers, Clover had been fascinated and disappointed. She had a passion to be where things were happening; Clover liked the centre of the vortex, even if the spinning and whirling of events practically knocked her off her feet.

When she telephoned Daniel, which she did every morning to talk about work and report on the previous day's research, she thought he sounded subdued. Positively dreary, Clover thought. His depressed voice was not the one she'd known for years, and she actually found it difficult to make him laugh – Daniel, who liked jokes more than any man she knew! Perhaps he wasn't well. Or not enjoying his work at Condaford; the relationship of designer and the rest of the company – director, leading actors, was such an ambiguous one. The play *had* to be designed and decisions *had* to be made, but sometimes the idea was so fluid, so ephemeral, that designer and director had completely different visions. Sir had never seemed to appreciate Daniel. Clover, who worshipped Sir like most theatre people, but was Daniel's devoted assistant, found herself with split loyalties.

It was matinée day, and most of the Ravenfield cars

were gone, but Clover saw Daniel's car in the stableyard. Helped by the taxi-driver, she dumped the back-breakingly heavy suitcase by Daniel's front door and ran up the stairs.

'Dan! Here's your mate!' she cried, bursting into the room at a rush. 'Glad to see me?'

Daniel was squatting on the ground working at an elaborate geometric design. He was using set squares and compasses and the thick cartridge paper was pinned to the floor to keep it flat. He looked up at her and couldn't help smiling. In a depressing world, here was somebody who did not change. Clover wore her jeans, her old sweater, her two silver chains, her air of cheerful humour, her affection for himself, just as usual.

'Great to have you back. Want to unpack?'

'Lord no! All my things are rolled up in my tote bag. I travel light. But the books *do* need unpacking . . . they weigh a ton. Can you get them, Dan? My arm's out of its socket.'

'Of course,' he said, springing to his feet.

When he'd gone, Clover squatted down and looked at the design. It was many-sided, many-angled, full of complex shapes and patterns; it was a kind of polyhedron. Staring at the lines until they made her dizzy. Clover thought: Dan looks *awful*. Quite ill. What's wrong with him? Is it me? Does he wish I wasn't back? Oh, that's damned silly, I haven't been around for days so how can I be the one who's on his nerves?

Clover, who was given to self-analysis, often asked herself if she bored or annoyed people. She did neither, but always thought perhaps this could happen. In Clover's world, the social crime was to be a bore.

Daniel came in with the huge shabby suitcase, and they unpacked the books together. His manner slightly altered and quickened with interest as Clover showed him her findings, discussed the illustrations, all of which she had carefully marked with long spills of paper and reference numbers. They talked about *Faustus*, and Daniel told her briefly what had happened at Condaford and how far . . . with Sir *hors de combat* . . . the production had progressed.

Kneeling on the floor, Clover said casually: 'You don't look so groovy. What's wrong?'

'Nothing.'

'Sir been picking on you?'

'I've scarcely seen him. He's convalescing.'

'Seen Julie around?'

'No.'

Clover made a grimace. 'Don't look at me like that, Dan Monteith! I can ask, can't I? *I* thought you and Julie got on rather well together.'

'Clover, don't be an ass.'

He stood up, opening one of her books. It showed a large-scale drawing of a magician, rolling his eyes and waving his arms grotesquely, and Clover had written: 'Guess who?' on the paper marker. The figure did have a certain comic similarity to Robert Waring.

But Daniel did not smile.

'Oh dear,' she said, with a touch of asperity. 'Not funny? *I* thought it was. What's the matter with you today?'

It was obvious that he did not want to talk about himself but Clover had known him a long time and she was not easily put off. She jumped to her feet, pulled up the chair Julie had sat in the other day.

'You *like* Julie Woods, Dan,' she said, 'and I'm not surprised. She's sensational. So what's with you both?'

'Do shut up.'

'I don't want to. I'm only asking a question. This is *me*, remember? Why have you given Julie up?'

'I haven't "given her up" as you put it.'

'Then what –'

'Clover, I do wish we could talk about something else. But since you're set on hearing about it, it seems that Sir is going to marry his new star.'

'*What*!'

'Oh yes. And this isn't a rumour. She came over here and told me herself,' said Daniel, slamming the book on the magician's figure so viciously that dust flew from it. He shoved it into the bookshelf.

Clover said no more.

The talk turned back to work and they settled down to a detailed discussion of what was to be done in the next few days.

Clover finally left Dan, went to her own digs in the Music Director's flat to unpack, and got herself a lift into the theatre. She always felt what she described as 'itchy' until she'd established contact with the theatre; it was like going home.

The evening performance had started, the grounds were lined with cars. The theatre, shining with lights, had the unmistakable feel of a building packed with people. When the interval came, crowds streamed through the open doors and sauntered on the lawns under the chestnut trees.

Clover slipped through a door marked 'No Entry' and went up to Julie's dressing-room. She knocked. The actress's hoarse little voice called, using Sir's phrase : 'Come.'

Julie, wearing soldier's chain mail but without her surcoat and buckles, was sitting on a chair by the open window. Her sword, with its chased blade and jewelled handle, lay on a table beside her. She turned as Clover came in and said, 'Hallo. I thought you were Chris. Nice to see you back.'

'Nice to be back. When I come into the theatre I realize how much I've been missing it,' Clover said. 'How's Sir?'

She stood beside Julie, looking – and feeling – a little shy. The other girl's magnificent costume, her make-up enhancing eyes and mouth, the soldier's haircut, the chased sword, gave Julie an air of unreality and yet of power. Clover tried, looking earnestly at the actress, to get through the magical disguise to the real woman.

'Sir is much, much better,' Julie said. 'We're so grateful he didn't break his arm. Imagine. He couldn't have played *Faustus* and the whole season would have been ruined. He's being an awful patient.'

'Of course,' said Clover.

There was an awkward pause.

'I did call about something else, Julie. It's about Dan, as a matter of fact. Do you know if anything's wrong with him?'

'Wrong with Dan? He seems all right.'

Julie's voice was just a fraction too quick. Her face was pleasantly indifferent. She said, 'I thought he looked all right when I saw him the other day.'

Clover, who had come with suspicions, heard them confirmed. She said cheerfully, 'Well, I think he's *dreary*. I mean, he's usually fun and laughs a lot but when I got back this afternoon I thought he was dreary. Surely you've noticed?'

'I can't say I have,' said Julie, turning back to the window again.

And that was all Clover got.

Clover went back into the auditorium. She waited until the performance started, and watched for five or ten minutes, standing at the side of the dress circle. The play held her, as it always did; it was strange to see Julie, the girl she'd spoken to a few moments ago, transformed into the Maid, speaking in that sweet hoarse voice which now had the trace of a country accent, laughing, inspiring a King of France . . .

Dragging herself away from the performance, Clover left the theatre and took a second taxi to Ravenfield. She was usually adept at getting lifts, but this evening she decided to spend the money. She was in a hurry.

She went boldly to the front door of the big house and rang.

Harriet opened the door and when she saw Clover's familiar figure, in jeans and sweater, long black hair hanging and glasses shining, she was pleased.

'I *am* glad to see you, Clover. Ravenfield isn't the same when you're not around. Have you come to see Sir?'

'Yes, please. Any hope I can be fitted in?'

'Of course. There's been a planning meeting all the afternoon, isn't it mad?' said Harriet. 'He is supposed to be resting. However, the moment they left, Sir was immediately cross and bored. You're just what he needs.'

'I haven't brought anything – flowers – anything!' said Clover, suddenly feeling the responsibility of visiting the distinguished sick.

'Bring him some chat. That's what he relishes,' Harriet said.

They went up the stairs and down the long corridor. Harriet knocked, opened the door and announced : 'Here's someone to cheer you up,' and left Clover alone.

Sir Robert was lying in a chaise longue by the window which overlooked the lawns and formal flower-beds of the garden. He was dressed in a towelling dressing-gown, snowy white and thick, which set off his handsome bony face and dark, grey-flecked hair. His arm was closely bandaged and arranged in a blue silk sling.

'How good of you to call on an invalid,' he said, with the sardonic note to his voice which made her laugh. He pointed languidly to the chair beside him.

'Come and sit. I've been contemplating the garden. It is singularly hideous.'

'But I like rose-beds,' said Clover. 'They always remind me of Alice in Wonderland.'

'Ah. If there were a lot of chaps painting the roses and the Queen of Hearts shouting "Off with their heads", that would be something like a view,' he agreed. 'Well, Clover? How are my *Faustus* designs? How are my Act One costumes? Where's Monteith? Haven't seen him for days.'

'He's in the laundry room working his guts out,' said Clover promptly.

The loyal riposte had no effect on Robert who merely continued to talk shop, questioning her in his penetrating way.

Clover awaited her moment. She was courageous and she had made up her mind to do what she considered was right. Now, faced with her formidable opponent, she reflected coolly on the right time to say what needed to be said.

'You are somewhat distraught,' remarked Sir Robert, immediately aware of an infinitesimal lack of attention. 'There is apparently something on your mind.'

'Well . . . yes.'

He regarded her with a lazy expression. Lying in his white robe, his bandaged arm gave him the look of a man who had been wounded but who had undoubtedly triumphed. A duel, perhaps. His magnetism made it impossible for Clover not to meet his eyes.

'Spit it out,' he remarked.

'I came about Julie.'

His relaxed, lazy expression did not alter a jot.

'What about Julie? She's well. Blossoming, one might say. Quite the little star, one way and another.'

Clover drew a deep breath and leaned forward, her long hair two curtains on either side of her face.

'Sir Robert, she is *not* blossoming,' she said earnestly. 'Dan tells me that you and Julie – well, everybody seems to know about it, it's all over the theatre, so I suppose I can mention it – that you have asked Julie to marry you.'

He looked amused. He slightly narrowed his eyes.

'Something like that.'

'Has she said yes?'

'My dear child, you must not be impertinent,' he said indulgently. 'I forgive you as you've come to visit me on my sick couch but I really cannot discuss it.'

He continued to look at her with veiled eyes, hiding a smile.

'But that's just what I've *come* to discuss!' cried Clover, tact gone to the wind. 'You have asked Julie to marry you and she's gone all pale and miserable, and Dan's gone dreary too and now where are we?'

Robert Waring looked at her in complete silence. His expression altered.

'Are you telling me that my little – that Julie has fallen in love with Daniel Monteith?'

Clover gave an anguished groan.

'I *hate* coming here and interfering!' she cried. 'Sir Robert, I know it is the most awful, awful cheek and I do ask you to forgive me. But when I came down this afternoon I saw there was something very wrong with Daniel, he's so odd and withdrawn, he's like someone ill, it's quite horrible. I guessed what was making him look like that so I thought I'd check. I *know* it's none of my business but I went to the theatre and saw Julie in the interval. She was sitting in her dressing-room and, do you know, Sir, she looked just like Daniel. Do you think it stupid when I say she looked withered? She loves him. She does. She truly does. And he loves her. I *know* it. If you get her . . .' went on Clover, her voice beginning to shake as she sat despairingly facing the beautiful, silent man . . . 'if you get her, and you easily can because you're a *magician,* you'll get her because you made her a star. She'll be yours for that reason. A captive, in a way! It would be marvellous for you and she would act together and everybody would be pleased – will be pleased – except Dan and Julie herself . . . Oh! I'm sorry! I'm sorry!' she finished, clasping her hands. 'Forgive me!'

Sir Robert had listened to this long speech with a face which, because of its very shape and strength, could never lack expression. But he had shown neither grief nor anger and now, raising his eyebrows, he merely said : 'Clover, let us have less of the melodramatics. That will do. I am devoted to Julie and you must leave the little thing's welfare to me. I understand her. Now, could you tell Harry on your way down that I'm ready to receive the Rome call when it comes through?'

As if by a trick worthy of Faustus himself, the telephone rang that moment and Robert picked it up. He launched into lilting Italian, waving Clover from the room, a king dismissing a courtier.

Clover left the house and returned to work. She did not know what to make of her interview with Sir. She knew she must hold her tongue with Daniel and she was glad when he telephoned to say that there was so much to do they would have to work late into the night. She went into the laundry flat and settled down to work, wishing her heart would stop thudding.

In the big house, Harriet and her Italian girls were preparing a delicate supper for the star. Harriet laid the tray carefully and carried it upstairs.

Robert had lit the lamp beside his chaise longue and was reading as she came into the room. He put down his book.

'Harry. Come and sit with me, dearest girl.'

His voice, flexible as an instrument, had a particular tone when he talked to his sister; it was protective. She knew he loved her and in return the devotion she gave him was too large and he took it as his natural right; and that was the way Harriet wanted it. She put the tray on the table beside him and he said, 'I want to talk to you, Harry.'

She glanced at him in the subdued light; he looked pensive. Sad, almost. How could that be?

'Is it about Julie?'

'Yes, Harry, it is. I suppose you've heard, since it seems my affairs are common knowledge, that I asked the little girl to marry me?'

'I heard. But I didn't ask you about it. I thought you would choose your own time to tell me.'

He eyed her for a moment. 'Disapprove?'

'Not at all. She's a lovely creature. Talented. Sweet.'

'I thought so.'

'Thought? Have you changed your mind?'

He said, rubbing his chin, 'It seems the Maid of Orleans does not love me.'

She genuinely laughed.

'No, I mean it. She's in love with the Monteith boy.'

'That's impossible!'

'Harry, Harry,' he said, shaking his head. 'I know what you are going to say. That nobody whom *I* love could refuse to have me. You're too prejudiced. Much too prejudiced.'

She looked at him earnestly, seeking for signs that he was hurt. He met this grave examination of his face with a look of mockery.

'You're in love with her, aren't you?' she said at last.

'Yes. But.'

'But what?'

'Well, I was thinking . . .' he said, picking a piece of celery from his tray and crunching it between his teeth. 'Nothing is settled between Julie and myself. I talked to her about it, of course, and about how I felt for her. And she was very sweet and made me a sort of declaration. Something of the sort . . .' he said vaguely. 'But in a way . . . I'm not sure it would do.'

'If you want her you'll get her. You get everybody you want. Always,' Harriet said. 'Because I suppose everybody is in love with you.'

'Yes, if we want them, the old magic works,' he agreed, grinning. 'However, whether I wooed the little Maid or not, the fact is that when I *won* her, if she was even slightly hankering after someone else . . . that could be tiresome. Very tiresome indeed.'

'It couldn't happen.'

'You are hopeless,' he said, laughing. 'When it comes to the crunch, your loyalty is *outrageous*. However, if you think it over you'll see what I mean. I might find it very troublesome and it might make her into a bad actress; these things happen. I'll talk to her some more and let you know.'

He began to eat his supper and remarked, with his mouth full, 'I didn't tell you that Mario has got hold of that *fascinating* play for me . . .'

Julie and Chris had fixed to have supper together and they returned to Ravenfield after the performance, in a battered Mini which Chris – inevitably – had been lent by a new bird in the box office. 'Very dishy. And very kind!' said Chris. Julie liked being with Chris who, as well as being an old friend and a cheerful companion, was unchanged since her recent fame. Chris treated her as just Julie and that was comfortable.

They arrived at Julie's flat, Chris put on the late-night radio pop programme and Julie cooked bacon and eggs.

'All we need is Margery Wylie popping in to tell us she wants us immediately for a midnight rehearsal,' said Chris.

'Dear old Sheridan.'

Chris scoffed. 'Don't pretend you hanker for the old days when we never knew where our next pay packet was coming from. Look at you now. The girl star. And Sir in hot pursuit!'

'Don't.'

'Why not? He is.'

'I'd rather not discuss it. Tell me about the new girl who lent you the car. And *then* I want to know what you think about that concrete music or whatever that Rufus is doing for *Faustus*.'

Chris, whose talk was never difficult to deflect, started to tell Julie about his latest bird. The girl wanted to be in opera. Imagine! He was launched into the middle of a story when there was a knock at the door.

They looked at each other in alarm.

'Margery Wylie's spook,' whispered Chris.

Harriet's grey head peered round the door. 'I'm so sorry!

You're both in the middle of supper. I only came, Julie, to ask if you could pop in and say good night to Robert in a little while. Would it be a nuisance?'

'Of *course* not.'

'I'll go and buzz round Clover. I want to see what's happening to the *Faustus* designs,' said Chris.

When Harriet had gone they resumed their dinner but in silence. Chris couldn't keep it up for long.

'Julie!' he burst out. '*What* about us not discussing Sir! How can we NOT discuss him? Are you going to have him, girl? Are we to hear the peal of bells from old Condaford Rectory? Tell a guy. I'm your mate, remember?'

'I haven't decided *anything*!' She looked so tense that even Chris relented. He bent forward and kissed her.

'All right, all right, how you do hate a tease. Finish off your supper and go and kiss the old Demon good night. There's always tomorrow, as they used to sing in some corny old Thirties movie!'

Julie left him regretfully. She walked through the dark garden as she'd often done since Robert had been ill. Harriet had left the door ajar; Sheba, sitting in the hall, thumped her tail at Julie but didn't bother to get up. Julie went quietly upstairs.

Robert's door was open and there was a sound of harpsichord music.

She went slowly into the room. She was wearing the white dress with the lace, which she'd worn at the party after *Joan*. It suited her well but she thought it made her look too young. As she came towards Robert she felt, for a moment, that the sight of her seemed to hurt him.

He was still up, sitting in the chaise longue by the window.

'How is it with you?' he said, putting out his hand.

'I'm fine. How is your arm?'

'Better. See. I can grip things now. I can grip *you*.' He took her wrist in his hand. 'I shall be back at rehearsal in two days.'

'Don't do too much.'

'Why not?'

They both laughed.

He was looking himself again. He wore a thin maize-coloured garment, Indian in style, with a high collar open at the throat. He sat for a moment, looking at her with a half smile. Then, in the throw-away voice he used in comedy, he said, 'Well? Are we to be man and wife, you and I?'

156

She didn't answer and he appeared to expect this. He added: 'Or is it Daniel Monteith who is to get the little saint?'

Julie blushed scarlet. Even her ears went red.

'Of course not. How stupid.'

'Mm,' said Robert. 'Rum. I had an idea you were rather taken with Monteith. Eprise, as the French say. Come on, Julie. Look at me and tell me, straight, that you don't love the fellow.'

She looked instead at the powerful hand gripping her own.

'Well,' he said finally, 'you'd better confess it. You know how well I read you – like an innocent little book. A child's garden of verse! You love him, don't you? So why isn't the idiot courting you, as I've been doing?'

'He doesn't love me,' she said.

And then, to Robert's intense irritation during a scene which so far he had dominated, she burst into tears. For the next ten minutes Robert had to cope with a woebegone, sobbing girl, her arms round his neck, behaving much as Tamara and Candida had done during their own courtships. The interview turned upside down. From being lord, protector, king, and – of course – suitor, Robert mopped tears, lent handkerchiefs, listened to confidences, and promised fatherly help. He even rang the bell and ordered a sleepy Mia (never surprised to find actors in tears) to warm some milk.

When she'd been coaxed to drink the milk and mop her face, Julie was told to be off to bed.

'Calm down and leave everything to me. Remember. You do what *I* tell you,' he said.

The forlorn figure left the room, leaving behind a trace of delicate scent and a childish half-drunk mug of milk. It was only then that Robert's face looked, for a second, as if a shadow chased across it.

Julie didn't see Robert all next morning. She went into Condaford to meet a journalist for luncheon, and in the afternoon returned to her flat to read the film script Renfred had given her. Wearing her old black practice clothes, and feeling depressed, she lay on the strip of lawn in her small garden and tried to read.

Mia arrived a little later, bringing Julie a melting Italian smile and a letter in Robert's handwriting.

It said merely: 'I want to talk to you. Come to the terrace and have a cup of tea.'

It was signed 'R'.

Like Royalty, thought Julie, thanking Mia and saying she would come at once.

She looked in the glass to be sure she wasn't too untidy. However tender Robert was, he made sarcastic comments if she didn't look what he considered her best. Avoiding the front door, Julie went through the back gardens to get to the terrace.

The french windows of the big house were open; in the distance Sheba walked round, owning the place. The rose-beds were full of flowers and a sprinkler whirled a rainbow of spray in the warm air. When Julie came on to the terrace there was one man waiting. It was Daniel.

He was apparently waiting for Robert and when he saw Julie he said at once, 'Sir told me he may be some time. He's on long distance.'

'Oh.'

They stood awkwardly looking at each other.

Daniel said, 'Shall we sit?'

They walked on to the lawn and sat in chairs a little distance from each other. Daniel looked at her. In her old black velvet and sandals she looked small. Pale, and clever, and small, and sad.

'Sir told me that you and he – that he doesn't think perhaps you would be right together,' he said.

Julie said nothing.

What was the use? Their meeting was contrived. Sir had fixed it like . . . like some ridiculous conjurer, some do-gooder in a musical! She thought : I wish I could go back to my flat and read my script in peace.

'What are you thinking, Julie?' Daniel asked. He sounded different and she sighed.

'If I told you, you would think it unflattering.'

'You're wishing you weren't here and why can't I leave you alone.'

'Something like that.'

'Was I very rude the other day when you came to ask my advice?' Her air of exhaustion and absent-mindedness, her indifference, moved him. He thought : I've lost her. She's miles away. She's a marvellous actress and capable of deep feelings and they've died. It's my fault.

'You were angry. I understood that. I let you down,' she said. 'And you didn't want to hear about me and Sir. Why should you? What is it to you?'

158

'Everything.'

She stood up suddenly and walked away across the lawn to a path edged with formal rose bushes in tubs, the roses Clover had said were like Alice in Wonderland. She wanted to get away. From Daniel, from Sir, from herself. She felt exhausted. She turned her back on the house and stared fixedly at a round pink rose with a myriad of petals, stout as a little scented cabbage.

There was a step behind her.

'Julie,' Daniel said in a low voice, 'please look at me.'

'I don't want to.'

'I need you to, Julie. I want to ask you to forgive me.'

'Oh don't!' she exclaimed, still turning away from him. 'We can't be friends. Don't let's try. It's true I am not going to marry Sir, it wouldn't do. He is right, he is always right, he's a sort of miracle for me. But you and I can't be friends because I'm an actress. I *need* to act and I mind about it and I forget appointments and I'm a drag and I go into a trance and I can't help it! I thought you understood things like that. You are in the theatre. You are so talented. I *love* your work,' she said, turning at last and facing him with a stricken look. 'But we can't be friends because of the way I am and I can't change. You don't love me so why should you understand me? It was ridiculous of me to hope . . . to have hoped . . .'

She never had the chance to say more because he put his arms round her and kissed her passionately. They separated only long enough for him to say, 'Dear love! Dear love! I adore you!' and then they kissed again. Unconscious of the big house with its many windows, unconscious that they stood on the sunlit lawn as though on a stage, they stood kissing and murmuring broken words.

'Marry me,' he said. 'Please. Please. Please.'

'Yes. Yes. Yes,' Julie said, laughing and crying.

Lazily, with a studied grace and Sheba at his heels, a figure came walking towards them across the grass. A figure that always seemed to have a spotlight wherever he moved, dark-haired, graceful, with the face of a hero.

'Very nicely played,' Robert said. 'You see, I have shed my sling today and it is possible to embrace you both.'

He put his arms round them and drew them close.

'Perfectly timed, perfectly directed,' he announced. 'I shall keep my new star and you, my boy, will design us some of your brilliant costumes. And remember, both of you, that you have to thank Me for seeing into your hearts.'

He gave them a swimming glance.

'Oh yes. Yes,' said Daniel and Julie together.

Julie stood on tiptoe to kiss Robert, saying with love and gratitude : 'You do *everything* for me. You know *everything*.'

She did not know how her manner to him had altered. She did not know that she'd lost the trick of seeing into his mind. She did not know that from now on his power over them both would be the power he had over everybody, the love and admiration and dominance he claimed as his rightful due.

Sir knew it, of course.